SHOTGUNNED

SHOTGUNNED

•

Duncan Ross

AVALON BOOKS
NEW YORK

Library of Congress Catalog Card Number: 2001088061
ISBN 0-8034-9491-2

Published by Thomas Bouregy & Co., Inc.
160 Madison Avenue, New York, NY 10016

PRINTED IN THE UNITED STATES OF AMERICA
ON ACID-FREE PAPER
BY HADDON CRAFTSMEN, BLOOMSBURG, PENNSYLVANIA

This one is for Kent and Britt

Chapter One

Kane Randlett kicked his mount out of the draw and joined the road. The big iron-bottomed grey snorted his approval. He was glad to be free of the hoof-sucking mud that had lined the ravine they'd traveled for the last few miles. Randlett smiled, hooked the reins around the saddle horn and patted the grey's shoulder.

The rays of a white-hot sun ricocheted off the roadbed forcing Randlett to pull a sweat-rimmed hat lower over his squinting eyes. The eyes were a pale blue that made his long black hair seem even darker. He was a tall, wiry man with skin brown as tanned leather.

He wore a faded red shirt with one sleeve—the sleeve of his missing left arm—tucked into worn buckskin pants. His saddle was Indian-made. On it hung a circular Howan garnished with grizzly bear claws . . . a glory-amulet from days past.

Randlett kneed the gelding to a fast canter on the hard-packed road. He was in a hurry now. He wanted to get this business over. He didn't like towns. City folk made him uneasy. And even though he had doubts about the rumors Draper had heard, the need to follow any lead still burned in his gut.

He rounded a curve in the road and was in sight of the scattered boulders called Big Rock that guarded the chasm over the pass. Suddenly the grey slowed. His small ears danced forward, trying to catch a sound on the wind. Randlett let him stop, then he sat listening for the rattle of buggy or clomp of hoof along the road. Nothing. He urged the gelding on, but the grey was tense, jittery.

Randlett's hand dropped to the butt of the Colt forty-four at his side. The big horse had never been wrong about trouble.

Circling around the strewn boulders, Randlett clamped his knees in an abrupt halt. A sharp pain clutched his stomach. A shiver ran down his neck as a distant almost forgotten feeling passed over him, a feeling he had experienced before. Sometime. Somewhere.

With sweat breaking out on his forehead Randlett urged the snorting grey closer until he recognized the debris clearly—a wrecked stage sprawled over the roadbed, its spilled cargo bloody and quiet in the steaming mud.

Shaking off a chill, Randlett sucked in a long breath and clucked the gelding ahead. Pistol drawn, he eyed the edges of the road, and when he saw the bodies sprawled the other side of the coach his chest tightened and his head swam.

He sang out a "Hello!". When no answer came he slid out of the saddle to study the carnage. The stage had toppled over, splintering an axle. The horses were tangled in the lines, one standing hip-shot, a bullet wound in its hind leg.

One man lay face down in the mud, shot in the back. Another had been dragged by the stage but he too had been shot . . . in the face. Another, a young man, had a deep red hole in his neck.

"Damn," Randlett muttered. His gaze searched for tracks near the bodies. Except for scuffling traces the team had made in an effort to break free after the attack, the ground was clear of prints. Rain had washed it smooth. Surveying the edges of the road, Randlett realized there would be no tracks to follow. The rain had been heavy and long during the night.

Wiping salty sweat from his lips, Kane Randlett leaned against the stage staring glumly at the horror. He felt tired. Nightmare remembrances floated through his brain as he recalled this same scene in another place, another time. Visions of running, of blood, of screams, brought a tremor to his whole body.

A low moan came from under the coach, startling Randlett into cold alertness. Wagging his head to bring himself back to the present, he knelt beside the buggy.

The white face of a steely-eyed cowhand glared up at him, one hand reaching as if for help. "He . . . he shot me," he muttered, "Didn't need to . . . didn't need to."

Randlett stared at the grim spectacle. Small holes, gouged in a circular pattern over the man's face and chest, oozed a steady trickle of dark fluid. The man groaned and moved slightly, trying to speak again. Randlett strained to hear but the pale lips merely trembled with the effort. Exhausted, the man slumped back into the mud.

Randlett put a finger on the man's throat and shook his head in disbelief. Still alive.

Randlett studied the limp form then turned, glancing with a sharp pain in his chest at each of the other bodies but knowing they carried single gunshot wounds. The others were shot with handguns or rifles. Only this man . . . one out of the whole crew . . . was shot with a shotgun!

His mouth a tight, thin line with fiery glints of anger sparking his agate eyes, Randlett swore, "Lord! Draper was right. He *has* started. . . ."

Randlett stood with slumping shoulders, his right hand unconsciously rubbing the empty left sleeve of his flannel shirt. He closed his eyes, dreading the truth but having to say it.

"Leek Fetty is on the kill. Again!"

The wounded man would never last into town on the back of a horse. Randlett needed to make a rack. He unhitched the team from the stage and drove three of the horses into a gully under a stand of timber. There he put the one that was hip-shot out of his misery with a bullet between the eyes. The strongest of the team, a patient bay mare, he kept for the travois.

From a couple of young saplings growing next to the ravine, he fashioned two stout side poles and laced a rope between them to form a stretcher-bed. Across this he laid several coats which he found among the passengers' belongings.

He worked swiftly and without thinking, his eyes covering the edges where a sign or trail might show. The gang had a good fourteen hour jump and the unbelievable good luck of the rain. But Randlett had no doubt he could find their trail if only he could take off now . . . not bother with the wounded man.

Tracking would require several hours looping in a semi-circle, guessing they would head north. South was a dry, flat desert with little water and no hiding places.

East was a possibility, but an area too well travelled. And if he remembered anything about Leek Fetty, it was the man's uncanny ability to be swallowed up in canyons and mountain crannies amid the wild breaks of the hill country.

Damn the man! A shudder of rage swept over Randlett as he thought of what might be happening all over again. And this time with the boy.

Mounting the grey, he took up the lines and led the mare, pulling the travois slowly into Wolfe City.

He was met at the edge of Main Street by two barefoot boys who excitedly pointed the way to Doc Monroe's office over the saddlery. Breathless, they ran ahead to tell their news to the sheriff.

Shyly noting Randlett's empty sleeve, several bystanders lifted the wounded man and carried him up the steps. The doctor, a small bespectacled man with short, swift fingers, examined the patient then wrinkled his pointed chin. "Won't make it," he prophesied.

"We need him to talk, Doc." Randlett soberly waited as the doctor again listened to the man's breathing.

"I'll let you know, but that might be too much to hope for."

"Thanks, I'll be checking," Randlett said as he turned to leave.

Outside the door of the office, he paused to survey the town. He studied the stores along the wide-planked boardwalk. He'd never been to Wolfe City. When the sheriff had sent for him he'd been surprised. He'd never had contact with the man—didn't know this particular sheriff at all. But he knew others. He'd made it his business to know many law officers these last few years in order to be ready for just such a lead as this one.

Randlett ran his hand over the soft leather holster at

his side. A strange dread was building inside him. A dread he'd never felt before. What was wrong? Were his old Cheyenne ideas about towns affecting him? Surely not. His feelings about crowds and 'whites' and towns had not interfered with the job of chasing other outlaws, or even Fetty those seven years ago. But then, he'd been a boy of seventeen and only one of a posse after this bunch. Probably too angry then to feel *anything*. Now he was alone and determined to see the chase through to the end. This time if it failed it would be on his shoulders.

Midway down the street he caught sight of the word Sheriff painted in tall red letters. Tipping his hat back he began walking toward it.

The day was a weekday. He was thankful for that. There was no Saturday glut of 'friendly' folk raring to bend his ear with questions.

Suddenly Randlett's chin lifted. A familiar, short, square-shouldered figure stepped into the street down near the Whoa Boy Saloon. If it was who he thought then the rumors might be true that Fetty had taken up robbing and killing around Wolfe City.

Randlett picked up his stride to a good clip.

In front of Bate's Dry Goods he side-stepped around several packing barrels stacked head-high on the walk. As he lurched back into the aisle he collided with someone coming out of the store. Randlett grabbed the slim form to steady it. In turn he felt small, strong hands clutch at his shirt. The hands stopped, fluttered in midair as one touch his empty sleeve.

The slim figure was a girl. "S . . . sorry," Randlett sputtered. Then smiled, hoping to make her embarrassment easier. People always made a big to-do over the missing arm.

The girl—woman, now that he looked at her—stepped back, ready to do her own apologizing. Then her head jerked up in surprise. She stood glaring up at him. She looked terrified, or startled, he thought, as her eyes widened.

Her long hair, which instantly fascinated Randlett, was grey. A silver-grey like bright moonlight on a fire's ashes. And it was pinned back from her face and rolled into a bun at the back. A few damp wisps curled over her cheek and dropped down across the curve of her neck. It was a long, regal neck that reminded Randlett of an elegant seabird he'd seen once on Green Mountain Lake.

"You. I thought you were . . . oh, I'm sorry," she continued. "I was in too much of a hurry."

Packages had scattered when they bumped and she accepted those he retrieved from the walk. She thanked him, keeping her gaze riveted on his face. He had never been scrutinized so thoroughly by a complete stranger . . . especially a woman. It made him uncomfortable. But then he couldn't help staring at her. Her eyes were blue, or green, with gold and orange flecks. Strange, he thought.

Smoothing the waist of her bodice over a long, full skirt, she wished him a good day and walked toward a buckboard tied to the rail. In one easy move she climbed up, slapped the reins over a saucy black gelding and moved off down the street.

Randlett headed again for the sheriff's office. But now his mind wouldn't focus. He could still feel the cool, bare flesh of her arm under his hand. The encounter disturbed him. He was used to being stared at. A one-armed man was always an item of curiosity or pity. But her steady gaze had been neither curiosity nor pity and he had a shaky feeling about it.

As he watched her buggy roll down the street he was surprised to see her wave at his square-shouldered friend who now leaned against the post in front of the sheriff's office. It was Bainbridge all right. Randlett smiled, then realized sheepishly as he watched the girl wave that he hadn't said more than "I'm sorry."

Randlett was greeted heartily by his friend who wore a deputy badge. Lon Bainbridge was an old hand at lawing. He'd served many times as a deputy. He'd been with the original posse that Randlett had joined seven years ago to go after the Fetty gang. Randlett was glad to see him and they entered the sheriff's office together.

Chapter Two

"You the reason Draper sent for me?" Randlett queried Lon as they waited for the sheriff to finish ordering a detail to guard the stage and its 'unfortunate' remains.

"Durn tootin'," was Lon's enthusiastic reply. The years had not been good to the aging deputy. The constant pressure and anxiety that went with trailing and bringing to bay a lifetime of ne'er-do-wells had put sagging pouches under his eyes. A constricting band of pain hugged his left chest and he put a hand there as he answered.

But his eyes gleamed with that old 'fire of the chase' as he added, "Draper can use you, Randlett. And you need a home base. I knew you'd find out sooner or later 'bout Fetty and I knew you'd want to be in on the fight. Sorry you had to find out in such a surprisin' way. You say you brung in a survivor?"

"Yes . . . but Doc thinks he may not live."

Lon Bainbridge sat down, his arms resting on his knees, his fingers laced together. He frowned at his dry, stubby hands and said with restrained affection, "I wanted you with me again Kane. We'll nail him this time."

They were both silent. Then Lon said, "Fetty's holed up somewhere in the Fox Tails. I'm sure of it. Signs tell it. You know that country is full as a rat's nest of renegade injuns, Blackfeet mostly but your own Cheyenne as well." He glanced at Randlett at the mention of "those" red men and Randlett nodded faintly.

The sheriff was still mumbling to the two men who would investigate the stage hold-up—one a pimply-faced kid, the other a whiskey-doused freeloader.

Lon said in a whisper, "Scalps fly outa them hills right and left ever time a sucker traipses in. No white man can git through that circle of injuns, Kane." He glanced at Randlett and added, "But you might git past 'em, boy."

Randlett quietly watched Lon roll a cigarette and promptly begin to wheeze and cough as the smoke flooded his lungs.

When the sheriff finished his instructions he turned to Lon. "This him?"

Lon took a deep raspy breath. "It's him. Kane Randlett meet Will Draper."

Randlett guessed Draper was near forty. He had coal black hair slicked back with some sweet-smelling greasy stuff. He wore a tailored grey suit and he kept turning his fingers up to study a set of newly-buffed nails. His skin was pale. As if he'd been living in his own jail cell, Randlett thought.

"I didn't know if you'd get my message, Randlett. Lon told me to send it to some old geezer named Tomas Thorne living in the Palucki Mine. But I guess it got to you since you're here."

Randlett stuck out his hand and Draper shook hesitantly, staring at the empty left sleeve.

"Don't worry 'bout that, Will," Lon Bainbridge assured him. "What most men can do with two hands, Randlett does better and faster with one." The deputy blew smoke then pushed the butt into a fancy blue ashtray on Draper's desk. "Ask the Batson brothers," he said and looked at the sheriff straight and long.

"You do that?" Draper shot back, his eyes squinting in disbelief. The Batsons had run through five counties, downing four lawmen over a two year period. The man that stopped them had been up against a clever cross-fire ambush from their own hideout. Draper knew that each of the brothers had met his maker with a forty-four slug dead center between the eyes.

"Well, I can use another gun. Lon says you two have already gone at Fetty . . . how long ago? Seven, eight years? I was in Missouri then so I'm not familiar with Fetty's previous skirmishes. But it seems from all I can learn he uses the same tactics of robbing wagons or stages, letting his boys rip up all the passengers. Just always saving the last—or at least one poor soul—for himself and his fancy shotgun."

Unaware of the concern on Kane Randlett's face the sheriff began to shuffle papers on his desk. He fingered them carefully, making sure the folder on top was aligned with the one underneath.

That done to his satisfaction he stood up and pointed to a map on the wall. "We think Leek Fetty is living somewhere around Wolfe City." He waited for agreement, got none and added, "Actually he may be, just possibly, one of our own ranchers, or businessmen, coming in to town innocently after his killings." Draper thumped the map with a long white finger.

"Ah, dangit, Draper," Lon stammered through a hacking cough. "Not this guy. He's leadin' a mad-dog bunch of shysters which he's gotta control and keep track of. I tell you he's. . . ."

"My deputy disagrees with me, Randlett, as you can see. He wants to begin tracking immediately. He thinks the gang may be hiding in the north mountain area right in the middle of the Blackfeet . . . at the edge of the raiding territory of that savage, treaty-breaking Cheyenne, Tom Stalking Deer."

Randlett smiled thinly on hearing that name and seeing the consternation it seemed to cause the sheriff.

Sheriff Draper continued, "I believe we need more information before we 'leap'. We'll wait, keep alert and be ready. This Leek Fetty will somehow show himself. Then we'll be able to pick him up or uncover his whereabouts. He may be doing business right under our noses."

Randlett plunked himself down onto a wooden bench under the window and angrily flicked a daub of mud from his boot. "Got any reports of a kid . . . or a young man being in these hold-ups?" He threw a quick glance at Lon.

"No," Draper answered, eager to spill all the facts he had. "We know there are usually four, sometimes five guns. And there is rumor of a huge red-bearded man with an Irish name. And whether it's true or not, one of the horses is an Appaloosa stallion."

Randlett scowled. "An Appaloosa?" Lon nodded agreement.

"Also," the sheriff went on with his information file, "they seem to strike only when there is enough cargo to make it profitable. The wreckage you saw this morning contained the payroll box from the XRT. That's why I've got Lon here riding all the incoming stages from now on. At least over that treacherous pass which is just an invitation for a holdup." Draper sat down in his leather chair.

Bainbridge shook his head, disgusted, and motioned Randlett to leave with him.

"Before you go, let me deputize you, Randlett." Draper opened a drawer and removed a jewel case. Inside lay a new gold badge on a pad of blue velvet.

"No thanks, Sheriff." Randlett followed his friend to the door.

Draper pushed up from his chair. He came forward to face Randlett. "Then why did you come all the way to Wolfe City? Why are you interested in chasing this gang again and not even getting the pay of a deputy. Why, you must not have been sixteen when you two went after Fetty the first time!" Draper's face was flushed.

"Seventeen. I was seventeen, Draper. Fetty only ran his gang another couple of years before he quit . . . or disappeared, so I didn't get a real chance at him. Never thought to hear from him again. But it seems he's taken up his old ways and I mean to get him this time."

Draper looked confused.

"You see, Sheriff," Randlett pulled his hat on, "I was one of Leek Fetty's first victims."

Draper scowled with listening eyes. Lon scuffed his boot toe at a crack in the floor.

Randlett continued, "My family was traveling to a new homestead in the Tall Pine Valley when I was thirteen. We had several wagons loaded with all the goods we possessed, including some jewels and family heirlooms. We were tracked for days before they hit but we were helpless anyway. Had no guns or knowledge of how to use one. The gang rode in on us and began gunning down my family. Seems they couldn't find all the money they thought we had and were some riled about it.

"They shot two servants, then got my ma in the back. Put a rifle slug into a cousin's face." Randlett's eyes laid a faraway gaze on the sleepy town framed by the window. His voice was a soft drone. "They turned on my pa and me then. Killed Pa with four slugs from a carbine."

Kane Randlett noticed Lon juggling for a smoke and he wondered why it should bother the old man after all these years. For Randlett it was just cold facts. "That Appaloosa stallion rode up then and Leek Fetty blew off my arm with his shotgun."

"Oh, gr. . . ." Will Draper bleached chalk white under his close-shaved beard. Clearing his throat he managed, "How. . . ."

"A band of Cheyenne found me." Randlett tightened his hat on his head and added, "They nursed me, gave me a home for the next four years until I left them to hunt Fetty. I met up with Lon here and we trailed together but never could find the bushwhacker."

Sheriff Draper regained his color and suggested, "So you want revenge."

"No," Randlett's voice was steady. "That's not my reason for wanting Fetty."

"Then what is your reason, pray?" Draper demanded, his forehead creasing in bewilderment.

"Fetty killed my family and blew off my arm, but he took a likin' to my nine year old brother. Yanked him up on his grand, spotted-rumped stallion and carried him away. Dragged him off screamin' and clawin' and fightin' mad . . . begging all the while for me to save him."

Draper was speechless. Randlett touched his hat and he and Lon walked out into the blazing sun.

Chapter Three

Wolfe City had dug in. From noon until sunset during these days of scorching mid-summer heat the air was stifling, heavy, dry, and hot. It burned the nose and if a man stirred himself his body wore a greasy mantle of sweat that added to his discomfort. Shutters were pulled and people stayed home.

The few storekeepers tending their wares retired to dark back rooms or sat dully in chairs pulled in front of the open doors where they waved the few stubborn customers to wait upon themselves.

"Can we get grub at this hour?" Randlett asked and Lon thumbed toward Delmonico's a few hundred yards away.

The large dining room held a dozen tables with a half dozen men sprawled here and there, each trying to keep a cool distance from the others. Heads swiveled and curious eyes stared as Lon and Randlett trooped through the room. The wild, back-woods look of Kane Randlett, even in a one-shot town such as Wolfe City, was noticeable. A man with one arm wearing a tied-down Colt in a handmade, raw-skin holster, drew attention even from the hardcases.

This was one reason Randlett felt uncomfortable in towns. He wished now he was free to ride out . . . back into the open range. At least there was a breeze there. The heat was beginning to get to him. It seemed breezes were creatures of the wilds. They didn't like to fool around city life any more than he did.

The urge to bolt was nearly overpowering within the close walls of the room. Until Randlett glanced at the deeply lined face of Lon Bainbridge. Randlett saw in a sudden flash an aging man who had already put aside the hard life of the law only to come out again when Leek Fetty appeared on the scene. His faithful friend was living on sheer gut determination. Randlett smiled to himself thinking he could stand a little heat after all.

The two men headed toward a back room where heavy drapes held some of the morning coolness. Randlett ordered steak and stewed potatoes. The waiter, aghast at the idea of firing up the iron stove, flatly refused. They argued until the waiter agreed to serve cold mutton and cold spuds . . . with reheated coffee. Lon swore that drinking hot coffee made a body cooler. The waiter 'humpfed' disgustedly and grumbled on his way back to the kitchen.

He was back with a tray of sliced meat and thick brown bread which he plumped beside a pot of slightly warm coffee. Lon tasted the tepid brew and turned a sour lip.

Randlett slapped a slice of meat onto one of the hunks of bread. He grew serious and said, "I don't like Draper having you ride escort for those stages, Lon. Can't you get out of it?"

Lon shrugged. "Draper figures it'll stall 'em off. Goin' on the idea that Fetty lives in town and knows what's goin' on o'course. Draper's a darn fool!"

"Well, every man works his own way but I figure he hasn't done much tracking sitting behind a desk all day."

The deputy nibbled at a piece of meat and asked pointedly, "Kane, you think you remember what Fetty looks like after all these years?"

"Probably not," Randlett said easily. "He was ugly of course but that might be because of what he was doing rather than how he really looked. He was an ordinary size I know, and there was nothing about him to mark him different."

Randlett bit into his sandwich then downed a cup of lukewarm coffee. He pushed his plate back, his face settling into cold, rigid lines. "I might not even be able to recognize Simon."

Randlett wiped his mouth, clicking his tongue at the loss he still felt when he thought about the boy. "Simon was a tough little kid, Lon, who could smile his way out of neck-high trouble. He had a face full of freckles and a way of moving like he owned the world. Of course Simon and Pa never got on. Simon was right sassy at times. Always did leave his chores for me to finish, I remember."

Randlett tried a tight smile, his desire to find the kid rekindled as he talked. "But Simon was my baby brother. I was responsible for him. The one really important time I had a chance to care for him, I couldn't. I aim to find him, Lon."

The older man sighed. Randlett looked up, sensing the deputy's feeling that he was overly conscientious about Simon. But Lon hadn't been there. Hadn't heard those screams.

Lon stirred his cold coffee and asked, "You reckon Simon's still being held captive by Fetty? He's now a growed man hisself, Kane."

"Yea, I know. But there are all kinds of ropes, Lon."

The deputy took out the makings and rolled a smoke. "That why you asked if a young'n was ridin' with 'em?"

"If Simon hasn't been able to break away, then he's being used, forced by some blackmail scheme, or through some other intimidation, to stay with the bunch. Fear maybe. . . ."

Lon drew an angry lungfull of smoke. His white forehead turned red and he lashed the table top with a burly fist. "Hell! Why in tarnation did that 'ombre have to start this business again."

Randlett answered calmly, knowing his own rage was not far from the surface. "I don't know, Lon, unless Fetty needs money. Like most outlaws, he has no spirit for working. Stealing is the only thing he's expert at. If Draper is right about the red-bearded Irishmen, Fetty has rounded up a new gang. I'd remember one like that."

"And that gun, Kane, you suppose it's the same?"

"I'd bet on it. A silver-monogramed gunstock is one you'd likely take care of and if my memory isn't playing tricks I recall staring long and hard at that handle when Fetty pointed it at me. It was daylight and the sun glittered off a big ol' F right before my eyes."

Randlett laid a coin on the table. "Let's check with Doc. Maybe that passenger is coming round."

The upper room in Doc's place was sultry. Acrid fumes of chloroform and alcohol mingled with the heat. The doctor was not in but Lon paid no heed. He walked through the open door and went over to a cot in the corner.

A girl sat next to the patient, fanning the air as she bathed the man's face with wet cloths. The sick man breathed in irregular gasps. The bandage on his chest was spotted with blood from the thumbnail size punctures.

Lon laid a rough hand on the girl's shoulder. He spoke gently. "Abby, this here's Kane Randlett. He needs a say with. . . ." He nodded toward the cowboy.

The girl glanced up at Randlett who towered uncomfortably tall in the little room. She was the girl he'd bumped into on the boardwalk. Lon stepped back to give Randlett his place. "This is Pat McMillan's gal, Abigail," Lon explained. "Mac runs the Double-M spread over on the Yellow Cat. She helps Doc nursing when he's got a hamstrung patient like this."

Kane Randlett wished the girl were not here. He suddenly realized he'd never been in such close quarters with a white woman since he was left on the trail for dead—certainly never one such as this, one that he'd touched. He felt awkward. Couldn't think what to say.

As he stepped beside her he noticed the finely-curling ash-blond hair was struggling out of the large bun on her neck. The hair looked soft, fragile. He didn't remember hair being soft. The inky blackness of Magpie's long tresses was always stiff with blunt ends.

And now as Abigail McMillan rose close to his chest he caught a whiff of . . . what? He blinked trying to remember the smell that rose from around this white girl. The smell too was a thing he'd not been around since childhood. Magpie carried about her strongly curved figure the natural odors of woodsmoke and bear grease, and the pungent odor of paint from berries or Seepwillow. This Abigail had no such 'natural' smell. Instead, Randlettt now recognized the faint odor to be jasmine. Stuff they called perfume, he guessed.

He was distracted and he didn't want to be. He needed information. Jaws grimly set, he waited as Abigail touched the man's hand and spoke him awake.

Surprisingly, the wounded man opened his eyes and looked up, moving his lips. Randlett leaned over. "Can you tell us anything, Mister?" Randlett found his own voice gravelly with emotion. "Was there a kid . . . a young man in the gang?"

"Yea . . . in the rain I . . . I did see a young'un. He never came close though. . . ." The cowboy moaned and sweat ran down his chin. But he wanted to talk and he managed, "A greaser . . . damn Mexican with . . . with a red silk shirt . . . he grinned and shot Miller in the . . . oh, Lord. . . ." The words faded and the man licked his lips. "An there was a little runt of a man smokin' . . . and a big one with a funny way o' talkin'."

Randlett leaned back to let Abigail wipe the man's now bleeding face. He bent close and asked, "The man who shot you . . . did the gun have a fancy stock with scroll-work on it? Could you see?"

The man managed a snort. "Yea . . . sorta . . . it shined up in the lightnin' like . . . like the devil's own. . . ." He drew a deep breath and added, "Appaloosa . . . rode a big Appaloosa. The snake shot me. Didn't need to shoot me . . . robbery was over. . . ." His eyes rolled and his head dropped.

Randlett turned aside, struggling not to see the images again. He stood as Abigail covered the man with a sheet.

She beckoned the men out the door.

The minute they were outside Randlett asked Lon, "Isn't there a Mexican village a few miles south of here?"

"Ojo de Agua," Lon said. "Not big enough to spit in. You thinkin' they might hole up there?"

"I'm thinking a fancy-dressed Mex might find it a pleasure to visit there with his pockets full of money."

Abby McMillan stepped close and studied Randlett, her green eyes shaded under her hand. "You a deputy too?"

"No, ma'am. Just mighty interested in finding this one party."

"You're not from around here." Her eyes traveled to Randlett's buckskin pants with their slim strips of fringed leather, took in the colt in the holster that had no real shape and finally came to rest on his lean, stubborn chin.

Lon interrupted, "Randlett ain't no city swell like your young man, Abby." He gave her a wink, but she frowned. "Don't worry, I don't tell everbody. He don't count." Lon ignored her discomfort and continued the description of his impatiently waiting friend. "This here 'ombre ain't set foot in town in a coon's age. Rather live next to them Cheyenne friends of his."

Then Lon turned serious and added, "Randlett has a real hankerin' to get Leek Fetty, Abby. An' he's got the iron to do it."

A tinge of worry passed over Randlett. He thought Lon's tired old eyes hankered, themselves, for that lost strength and know-how which he had once possessed.

Starting for his horse at the rail, Lon said heartily, "Well, let's go and scout out this Mex town."

Randlett stopped him in his tracks by replying, "I'm going alone, Lon. You hold the fort here. Keep your sights out for this Red-Beard Draper told us about . . . or the runt. And keep that sheriff pleased! We don't want him pulling against us."

Lon's shoulders slumped, then recovering, he vigorously shoved up his Stetson. "Yea . . . well, okay, boy. Guess you're right. But that Ojo de Agua dump is no place to close an eye in. Watch your step."

Chapter Four

Randlett headed for the livery. The grey was waiting. He'd been grain-fed, newly brushed and hayed, and he was ready to travel. Randlett spurred to a fast run.

According to the hostler Ojo de Agua was a three hour ride south. The plain dropped a mile out of Wolfe City into a dry, mesquite-riddled desert where the rocky alkaline soil supported a few spindly cacti and an occasional clump of sage.

Sun bleached the land. Turned it chalky, dried up the plant life. Anyone who traveled here quickly wished he had never had the idea. Randlett was no exception.

Now a magnificent sun, ripe as an orange, hung over the horizon as Randlett kicked the weary grey up a ridge covered with cholla. The horse was sweating heavily, his nostrils caked with smothering alkali dust. His breath wheezed and his muzzle was hot to Randlett's hand. He needed water badly.

His eyes a thin slit, Randlett scanned the desolate country on all sides. He dismounted, searching for shade.

He had ridden without let-up for three hours and the grey was too hot. Randlett was a man who knew the dangers this wild land could throw at a man. He knew its traps and its subtle risks. But he had not heeded his knowledge this time.

A knot of self anger rose in his throat. This was no way to begin tracking, riding off without thought or plan—and selfishly alone when it would have been no more bother to let Lon come. Had he let this crazy killer get under his skin so that he lost his common sense?

Randlett shook his head. It was just . . . just what? Just that he was swamped again with that same feeling he'd had in town . . . that same uneasy sense within that threatened to overwhelm him. Was it simply his worry over Simon? Must be, he told himself. After all, he had not really thought the boy was with Fetty until the cowboy admitted seeing a young man with the crew. The news had shaken him.

Randlett untied the nearly empty canteen. He should have stopped an hour ago and refilled it. He touched the canteen to the horse's lips, dribbling the water into his eager mouth. Then he mounted and toed the horse to a slow walk. Within twenty minutes they were gazing on a small hovel of a town.

A few low-slung adobe huts huddled atop a sand dune. Rickety corrals, holding a scattering of goats had been laced in between. Randlett studied the place a moment before he recognized the well. Large native stones had been piled in a foot-high circle around a small seep. It was to his left, before he would come to the buildings.

A single large mesquite tree guarded the well and a scrawny patch of weeds turned it into an oasis.

Ojo de Agua . . . eye of water . . . waterhole. Randlett nudged the grey. He hoped the water was sweet.

It was not. He raked away a green scum, cupped up a swig in his hand and sputtered it out onto the sand. The water had a rank, dead taste. It was alkali-laden. But it would not kill a man so he let the grey drink, pulling the balky head away to keep the animal from taking too much.

Randlett drank none himself, willing to suffer thirst for a day rather than get the scours.

Leaving the grey under the tree, reins tied to the slim trunk, Randlett sauntered up the sandy incline. His eyes roved the adobe huts and fence rows. His hand swept back and forth over the forty-four.

The largest adobe in the center had no sign. But its batwing doors opening into the dark recesses of a dirt-floored, vile-smelling room was sign enough. Randlett hesitated at the doors until the shadowy forms inside took shape. Then he walked in.

Warped planking was laid across two cracker barrels to serve as a counter. Three gnat-sized tables cluttered the small area. The place reeked with the stale odor of spilled beer. Randlett's nostrils were further assailed with the stench of rancid meat coming from the back room.

He strolled to the bar and waited while he glanced around. Three men sat at one of the tables drinking and sullenly flipping cards. One was young and bigger than the others. He was dealing. He did not look up. The other two watched Randlett with dark beady eyes that flicked back and forth to the dealer.

An ancient Mexican with no top teeth leaned behind the plank counter. He was mumbling to two white men. Drovers, Randlett surmised and waited for the old man as he made them a deal for a 'lady of the night'.

The old man took their coins and called for Arita. A

short, round-faced girl slinked in from behind a door of dangling beads and hooking an arm onto each of the men, led them out.

"Anyone speak English?" Randlett asked the barkeep. Although he knew some Spanish he wanted to keep the conversation in his favor.

His answer came from the card players. The dealer spoke with his head down, his hands shuffling out the broken cards with great care. "Some. What ees your beesiness?"

Randlett had planned his reply. At least he had enough forethought to do that. "Heard there was a silversmith in this area. Wondered if you boys might know 'im." The dealer showed no response and Randlett watched the old barman whisk a dirty rag over the plank. His face too was an unreadable mask.

"Seelver Smeeth?" One of the men asked in a doubtful tone.

"Yea," Randlett explained, "he can do fancy inlay work . . . with designs or letters. Probably works on saddles or rifle stocks and such." He let his information sink in and wished desperately he dared order a drink.

"Garcia," slurred one of the card players.

"Sí, old Garcia maybe you mean," the dealer affirmed.

Randlett was surprised. It had been merely a ploy, he had not thought such a connection would be in this hole of a town. He'd come strictly to find the red-shirted Mex the cowboy had noticed in the holdup.

"Can you tell me where he lives?" he asked with a frown of new concern.

"Shure . . . he leeves in the las house with the goats."

"Thanks," Randlett said and slipped a coin from his pocket. He put it on the counter and turned, adding, "You happen to know a man who wears his hair long and likes red silk shirts?"

Cards spewed to the floor. The dealer pushed his chair back at the same instant Randlett's hand moved to cover the forty-four. Fear flashed across the dealer's ruddy face and he quickly stopped his rise. Suddenly a grin spread over his face. "No, Senor," he said. "There ees no such 'ombre in Ojo."

Knowing the men would say nothing more Randlett went through the swinging doors.

The blue hills far to the northwest were black humps against a greying sky. The square adobe houses were numberless dice thrown on a grainy hill. The odor of woodsmoke floated on the sultry late afternoon air.

When Randlett heard the bleating of goats he hurried in their direction.

Passing several of the huts he noticed two men lounging in doorways. Neither wore a red shirt. Neither had long hair. From another adobe a baby cried. Randlett wondered where the drovers had been led.

The last hut on his right was Garcia's. Goats littered the front and sides of the dirt yard surrounding the adobe. A knee-high fence of woven brambles kept them from the other yards.

As Randlett approached, a small nanny popped out the doorway followed by a stoop-shouldered, thin little man whose skin was as black and wrinkled as a walnut. He stared at Randlett with one hand on the she goat's head.

"You Garcia?" Randlett asked in Spanish.

"Sí."

"You work in silver?"

"No more. Once I have done such."

"You ever carve a special silver stock on a shotgun?"

Randlett watched the old man's eyes narrow then he added, "The one I'm speaking of would have been made long ago . . . it had fancy scrollwork . . . with a big letter F on it."

The wrinkled Mexican hunched back into his hut, fear sparking his eyes. "Garcia make no more, señor. No more. No more."

A heavy sack fell across the doorway.

Disappointed that he would get no more information, Randlett was sure he'd stumbled upon the origin of the gunstock on Fetty's shotgun. There could be no other reason for the old man suddenly not wanting to talk.

Fetty must have known about this place and the man Garcia. Huh!, Randlett thought. Sante Fe was the place to get fancy silver work . . . always had been. But Fetty was a smart devil. Better to have such identifying work done in a place like this than in Sante Fe.

Randlett circled the village, looking neither right nor left. He wanted to stir up no more trouble. And it was time to wait for Red Shirt.

At the well he mounted up and set the grey to a slow cantor back the way he'd come. He rode only a mile before he came to a gravel pit. Riding through it he came out into a mesquite-riddled swale that would continue to cover his tracks. Out of this he swung back toward Ojo de Agua. This time approaching from another direction.

A high ridge on his right rose five hundred yards out of the earth. He eased up the side opposite the village.

At the top of the small hill he threw his bedroll, pulled the saddle and hobbled the gelding in a patch of pulpy saltweed. The gelding fell to, munching the greasy stiff grass. Randlett envied the grazing horse. A gnawing thirst had begun to govern his senses. Before morning he would be miserable. Sighing at his rashness, Randlett settled near a boulder that provided a view of the adobes.

The sun was setting and he was tired. But he intended to stay awake and watch. Those card players had not reacted to the idea of a red shirt for nothing.

Chapter Five

Not a soul stirred. A few candles glowed in some of the huts and two figures moved from one adobe to another. And later Randlett noticed a boy leading burros to the well. But he'd seen no one who looked like Red Shirt.

Two saddle horses stood behind the whiskey house—probably the drovers's—but there were no horses fit for a money-stealing bandit. Only a mule and three other burros. Had Red Shirt already gone?

Randlett chewed on a string of jerky, barely able to swallow, his mouth was so dry. Lon's hot coffee would be mighty welcome right now, he thought. The sun had long ago set but a soft glow lingered in the west. He squinted at the desolate little buildings. Still nothing. It seemed his idea the man would be spooked because he asked about him was not true.

Randlett sighed, arguing with himself, "If he *is* in the village he'll probably stay the night and leave in the morning."

Randlett decided not to spy any longer although he could see well enough when night came. While living with the Cheyenne he'd developed a good sense of night vision. The Indians trained themselves to see at night by not having a fire when on the hunt, instead allowing their sight to soak in the meager light from stars or moon or even the natural glow off sand and rock. Now a half moon rose, lighting his camp with a feathery softness.

And of course another possibility was the bushwhacker could slip away to the east. That side of the village was blocked to Randlett's view.

He pulled his ground cover from the saddle and laid it on the saltgrass. Then he wrapped himself in his blanket and shivering in the cold desert air, fell asleep.

He woke and turned over. Later he woke and listened in the darkness.

Still later he woke again, then dozed.

Once he strolled to the boulder and peered down at the village. It was quiet and dark.

Sometime before dawn in a murky, green haze, he woke suddenly. He lay still, waiting, tensed like a coiled snake. He breathed in a shallow, quiet rhythm. His senses were tuned to hear, to pick up air currents, to feel heat, to inhale the odor of intruders stalking the morning darkness.

The sliver of moon hovered behind low clouds and a wind blew across his feet away from the grey. The animal stood sleeping.

Randlett held his head rigid, only his eyes moved and they jerked cross-wind to his left, searching. His arm lay by his side, still but ready.

When the rank whiskey breath of the man near his head sent a responsive chill over Randlett's muscles he shot like an arrow from a pulled bow. His feet jackknifed his body to a flat-footed crouch, landing him beside the card dealer who held a pointed, double-edged blade over the empty blanket.

As Randlett clubbed him with a fist to the back of his neck he cursed and toppled over with a thud.

Movement behind whirled Randlett around. He froze as he gazed into the barrel of a forty-five and the sneering grin of a swarthy-skinned, long-limbed bushwhacker wearing a bright red silk shirt beneath a fringed leather vest. The Mexican stood cool and loose, this thumb easing back on the hammer of the big Smith and Wesson.

Randlett calculated his next move as he swept a quick sidelong glance to the groaning figure on the blanket. The man still clenched the knife in his fist. Randlett hadn't planned on killing. He wanted information and his hesitation fed the curiosity of the Mexican. He could not resist asking, "You wanted me, Injun man? Well, I am here." He motioned hands up and Randlett moved his hand away from his holster.

"Not you I want to see," he answered.

The man's hooded eyes leered. "No, señor?"

"I need to talk to your boss."

Red Shirt chuckled, then stopped, deadly serious. "Why?" he asked, cutting the word off sharply.

"We're old friends," Randlett stated. He could feel the dealer gathering himself up, advancing with the blade of the knife held out before him. ". . . and we need to talk business." Randlett's muscle's hardened.

"What beesness, señor?"

"Business that involves robbing and killing . . . slaughtering innocent people like cattle!"

The knife was at the edge of Randlett's vision. He needed to make a fast play if he survived. Then the gunman raised a hand to stop the knife wielder. "You have seen thees . . . robbing and keeling, señor?" he asked.

Randlett's jaded breathing slowed and he said, "One of your victims lived to tell about it. He testified that one of the killers was a Mex, wore a bright red silk shirt and a nice black vest. And had long hair."

The man's mouth twitched but he did not move.

Randlett went on, "And he mentioned your boss liked to shoot the last victim with his silver-monogramed shotgun . . . and ride off on his Appaloosa."

Now fear blazed across the Mexican's face. He held the forty-five with both hands, slowly sucking in a hissing breath.

Time was slipping away. At the man's next words Randlett was ready.

"Thee boss would not like what you say, White Breed!. . . ."

Fire blossomed from the leveled gun at the same instant Kane Randlett's hand dropped and came up firing. The Smith and Wesson's .45 slug tore a hole in Randlett's hat but the bullet from the Colt blew the incredulous bandit back into a low-growing cactus. He rolled over with a garbled scream, his face and hands full of barbs and a deep crimson splotch spreading across his forehead.

Surprise gave Randlett a split second leeway. He swirled, blasting the knife from the hand of the terrified dealer. Booting the blade aside, Randlett stuck the Colt's hot muzzle into the throbbing pulse of the man's throat. "Now!" Randlett's voice was tight as he pushed muzzle against flesh. "Where are they?"

The dealer's face was paste. He gargled his words, "I . . . I do not know. Pleese señor, I am not of the banditos. Believe me. I speak the truth on the grave of the Holy Mother. I know nothing of thees beesness."

Feeling the man's body quake, Randlett despaired. He was up against a dead end.

"Money, señor. Morales . . . he gave me money," the shaking man managed. He nodded at the still form of his partner. "He pay muchos pesos . . . heere." He delved into a pocket and held out a trembling handfull of grubby coins.

Randlett lowered the gun, holstered it, then grabbed the man by his flimsy shirt. "You never heard of Leek Fetty," he stated.

"Sí, señor. I theenk maybe Morales he works for thees bandito . . . for thees Fetty . . . but no one knows from where they come or go. Pleese, señor!"

"You ever see this gang?"

"See?"

"See the banditos with your own eyes. How many are there?"

"One time I see them, señor. Riding through . . . there were six I theenk. Sí, six."

A low whine escaped the man as his shirt split. Randlett's fist let go only to clutch the man's throat. "Was there a young kid, eighteen, nineteen, years old?"

"Purhaps," a torn whisper gurgled to the pale lips.

"What . . . what did he look like?"

"Nothing. I know no more señor. Pleese I know no more. He was like the others . . . American. Young and riding in the bunch."

Randlett shoved the man back toward the limp body of Morales. "Take your friend into town and bury him." Reflecting, he added, "Anyone wants to know, tell them Kane Randlett shot him. If anyone objects . . . send 'em to me."

He walked over to a bed of gravel. He picked up the knife, hefted it for balance. Frowning, realizing with a tingle on the back of his neck how close he had come to death he slipped it into the side pocket of his boot.

He turned and quickly saddled the grey. Without a look at the two men he rode out into the fresh cool morning toward Wolfe City.

Chapter Six

Deputy Lon Bainbridge stepped under the shade of the overhang in front of the sheriff's office. Struggling to keep a placid face, he raised a hand and pressed the tight band of pain over his chest. His eyes watered and he closed them for a second. Beads of sweat bearded his upper lip.

When the spell passed he went into the office.

"Oh, Lon, glad you're here. We have new information just in from Smoke Hill." Sheriff Draper tossed a letter onto the desk and sat back, gleaming about the way things were shaping up in the Fetty business.

"Marshall Spruett says one of the Fetty gang is an ol' timer with the handle of McPherson. Soda McPherson. Spruett thinks this McPherson joined the gang just recently."

"How come?" Lon wiped his face and sat down.

"Well, it seems he lived in a shack on the outskirts of Seelyville till a few months ago when he ups and leaves."

"That all?"

Draper smiled. "Oh, no. A friend of the Marshall spent a lot of time drinking with this McPherson and he claims McPherson was always bragging about 'makin' it big 'again'. Spruett's friend didn't think anything about such a brag until the old man purchased a brand new '73 Winchester, a one-hundred dollar saddle horse, and promptly left town."

Lon's hand shook as he lit a hastily rolled cigarette.

"You recall anyone by the name of Soda McPherson, Lon? Seems strange the old man would say, 'again', don't you think?"

"Ah don't recall anyone by that name as mentioned when we rode after Fetty first time . . . only name bandied about wus a Skeet Johnson and they found his body over in Arizona few years ago.

"But," Lon blew smoke and stood up, "they did say one of the gang was an ol' coot . . . a loyal-as-hades kind who'd do your stealin' and robbin' for you, shine your boots when you got home, and gladly hang hisself 'fore he'd squeal on you."

"Well, now we have one name of the gang and a good description of one of the others. We're closing in, Lon."

Lon concentrated diligently on the ashtray on the sheriff's desk. That huge marvel of cut blue glass was capable of holding a month's supply of butts . . . and as usual it was wiped as clean and shiny as a new spittoon. Lon leaned close and carefully squashed his lopsided cigarette butt over the entire bottom, making sure the smoke was good and out before he said, "Did the posse turn up any tracks?"

"Huh . . . no. Of course not. Didn't expect they would with the rain and all."

"And too," Lon drawled, "three part-time city dudes ain't 'bout to range too far and pick up any after-the-rain trail, not bein' able to get in for a hot supper if'n they did take out on such a expedition."

Sheriff Draper gave a sneer then spoke patiently, "I let you talk me into sending for this Kane Randlett fellow, Lon, and you see where it got us. Won't even let me deputize him. I'm afraid he merely wants revenge. That tale of a brother being with Fetty is pretty wild. The boy undoubtedly escaped long ago."

Lon stood silent, not giving a hoot to share the information the cowboy had given them about the gang . . . about a young man being with them.

Draper studied his watch and said, "The next stage I want you to meet is due Friday. If you wait for it at the pass and ride all the way in with it, I'll feel better."

"Any money on it?"

"Yes, there will be. Several thousand coming in to finance Gus Springer's building projects here in town. Only a choice few men know about the money." Sheriff Draper grinned.

"Why you happy, Draper?" Lon asked, his chest suddenly tightening.

"Oh just thinking of the little ploy I've set up by telling two of the local men about the incoming cargo . . . just on the chance one of them might slip and expose himself as one of the gang. Why, one of our own may even know this Soda McPherson . . . be his contact man."

Lon slammed the door when he left.

The Whoa Boy Saloon was the only cool place in Wolfe City. It was double raftered with a floor above the saloon itself. The building had a front and back door that lined up north and south allowing a breeze to flow through the center of the barroom. Large cottonwood trees shaded the south entrance making the breeze ten degrees cooler.

Kane Randlett scooted to a halt near the watering trough under one of the cottonwoods. He fell off the tall grey horse and made a dive for the pump at the end of the trough. As water gushed out he plunged his head under, turning his face aside to catch the cool, sweet liquid. He drank only a few seconds then lowered his hot, alkali-covered head and neck until he was thoroughly soaked. "Didn't think I'd make it, boy," he told the grey as he stood back and shook his long wet hair.

He took another drink, then smiling, drew the grey to the trough.

At noon the Whoa Boy was crowded with men trying to avoid the sun's stultifying heat. For a moment Randlett stood in the doorway looking them over. He spied Lon sitting at a table in the corner talking to a black-mustached cowboy.

Lon stood up as Randlett approached. "Any luck?" he boomed as demanding as a kid asking about his present.

Randlett grinned. "Some," he said and set his hat on the table as he pulled out a chair.

"Well, don't hold back on his account," Lon waved a hand at the cowboy who was one of those outdoor men who stay vigorous and agile all their life, never showing their age. Grey lightened the long sideburns and a frown creased his forehead, but he could be thirty or sixty.

"This here's Abby's pa, Kane. Him and me have been exchanging lies goin' on five year . . . since I been in these parts."

McMillan rose and shook hands with a withering grip. He looked Randlett in the eye and Randlett immediately trusted him.

"You see the Mex?" Lon could wait no longer.

"Yea . . . saw him. But he was unable to help me." Randlett sat back in the chair, letting his tired body relax.

"Was he one of 'em?"

"Seems so. Yea was." Randlett made it sound final.

"By jingoes! One down, boy. You get hurt?"

The old deputy searched Randlett's shirt and face, then his eyes rested on the burn hole in the dusty leather hat. Knowing the trouble had been real he said cockily, "Too bad his friends weren't there too . . . or was they?"

When Randlett remained silent Lon said with a low whistle, "Dang! Wished I hada been there."

"Red Shirt's name was Morales and he did have a friend but he wasn't one of the gang. He was a local, paid by Morales to point me out. But he came across with one piece of information. Said he saw the bunch once and swears there's six . . . says a young man was riding with them."

Lon stamped the table with a hearty fist. "Hallelujah! Now we're aiming true. The kid's there and we'll get him back this time.

"Huh," Lon nodded toward McMillan and added, "I've been tellin' him the sitiation, Kane. He's a good man to have on our side."

Randlett tipped back his chair and met the interested but unpretentious glance of Pat McMillan. "Okay by me," he said. "Be glad to have your opinion of how things go with the locals."

Randlett turned to Lon and lowering his voice asked, "You sure about the Fox Tails, Lon?"

"Bet my last pouch on it, Kane." Lon patted the tobacco sack in his shirt pocket. "I cal'cate they're past the Dripping Springs Cut—probably nesting right on top of Tepee. That there butte is a fair place to hide and keep alive in secret. Only way in is the Divide and as you know, them Blackfoot have control of it and all the territory 'round it . . . clean to the end of the Fox Tails."

"Then I'll need Stalking Deer." Randlett set his chair back on its feet and rubbed his neck in sudden concentrated thought.

"Draper's got Stalking Deer on his black list, boy. Better play it easy, keep your plans from sheriff ears."

"Don't worry, Stalking Deer wants to stay free, he'll not put himself in jeopardy. I'll be lucky to track him down."

Lon nodded at his friend and said, "Pat, here, has a good wrangle of hands who are willin' to help."

"Yes, I do, Randlett," Pat McMillan assured him. "I have two men who are more than fair guns. You're welcome to use them."

"Thanks," Randlett replied. "I'll keep it in mind. Right now we have to figure how to get through Dripping Springs and it won't be with gun play. Can't tangle with Indians these days or you'll find yourself in trouble with the U.S. government.

"What we need," he continued, "is luck, a lot of sweet ol' savvy, and the help of a red Indian by the name of Tom Stalking Deer."

Randlett stood up and pushed back his chair. "We'd better hit his trail. You comin' Lon?"

"Yea, yea, let's go." Lon eagerly rose, adding in a near whisper, "If Simon is bein' forced to ride with Fetty and then held in that devil of a place as a hostage . . . or prisoner . . . we'll shure have to play it careful."

The men walked out to their mounts to see Abby McMillan seated on a slim black mare. "Waiting for you, Pa," she hailed her father.

Randlett found himself staring. She was dressed in a tan riding outfit with a yellow waist. A broad-brimmed, tan hat shaded her smooth white face from the sun. Randlett was aware of his chalk-dusty pants and sweaty shirt and his long hair—cut Indian style with a knife—that was still damp.

"I trust you found the material you wanted, girl," Pat asked as they mounted up.

"Surely did, Dad. By the way, Mr. Randlett, you'll have to come to the dance next week. We have one every year after the late roundup." Abby McMillan flashed a brilliant smile.

Suddenly Randlett realized how much he had lost out on the normal amenities of "white society". He smiled wryly as he toed the stirrup. He couldn't waltz or do the Virginia Reel but he knew all the intricate steps of the Dance of the Buffalo. He was certain the cool Miss McMillan wouldn't appreciate his unusual skill so he said, "Thanks, Miss McMillan, but I'm not much for socials."

Lon stood by Abby's mare and patting her hand said, "Will that sweetie o' yours be there, Abby . . . for everbody to meet?"

"Yes, Lon. He's promised me this time." She looked at her father who clucked his mount, shaking his head as if he'd believe it when he saw it.

Lon turned to Randlett as he gathered reins. "She's got a secret feller, Kane, who shure is some sweet-talking 'ombre. Met him onct when I happened over to the Double M. I swear, he shure can talk you up from the grave. Whut wus his name now, gal?"

"Suede Carson, Lon." Abby smiled at Lon's description of her beau and then gave him instructions about his own attire for the dance. "You're to dance with widow Stanton, now, Lon, remember."

Chapter Seven

Father and daughter rode ten miles before they met the southern fork of the Yellow Cat. As they crossed the bridge and rode up to the long, rambling ranch house Pat McMillan called, "I'll take Lady and have Jake put her up, Abby. I know you're anxious to try that new recipe for gooseberry pie." His eyes crinkled and she laughed.

"Dad, you can always be so thoughtful when you've a reason."

But she did want to try the recipe. She was the cook now that her mother was gone and she prided herself on making the best desserts in the territory. "You be in before dark for a change, okay?" she called.

"If that fence is fixed on the west end." Pat McMillan slapped the black mare toward the corral and rode out to supervise the work.

Walking into the house, Abby felt her usual thrill of pleasure. She loved the cool, high-ceilinged hall with its polished sideboy and mirror. A bowl of asters sat on top of it . . . just as they had every summer since Abby could remember. It had been a hobby of her mother's to grow asters and arrange them for the house. Now Abby did it.

She dropped her gloves on the sideboy and went into her bedroom. She untied the ribbon around her hair. As she turned to pick up a comb a man leaped from behind the door and seized her in one engulfing swoop. He locked his arms around her waist, clamping her in a tight vise. Pressing his face to her cheek, he whispered in a mocking voice, "Captured at last . . . the elusive Miss Abigail McMillan. Now to ride away to the hills!"

Suddenly she relaxed and tried to turn. But he held her and began to kiss the back of her neck, "Suede," she sighed, half mad, half pleased. "What are you doing in my bedroom. If Dad catches you in here. . . ."

"Ah, but he won't now will he, my love?" Suede Carson was a muscular, black-haired young man whose self assurance left her speechless. He was never without an answer and his answers were for life and daring and excitement. No wonder she had been smitten from the very first time she met him.

"Let's go for a ride," he suggested with a broad smile and a wink. He pulled her toward the door.

"No, Suede . . . not now. I have things to do. Supper to fix. Oh, stay this time. Stay and have supper with us. You've only been with Dad a few times and he'd love to get acquainted. I'd like it too, Suede." She searched his handsome face to see the answer she desired but as usual his smile told her nothing.

He took her hands and kissing them said, "Someday soon, Abby. I promise. As soon as I've . . . I've straightened some things out that I owe. I'll be able to meet your Dad and ride into town with you, and we'll eat at the new hotel and I'll buy all the new dresses and bonnets and. . . ."

"I don't need new things, Suede." An icy chill crawled over her when he talked this way. She felt helpless. "I just want to be with you."

"That too," he assured her and drew her over to the window seat where they sat holding hands.

"What's new in the great city?" he asked as if they were an old married couple and she had been shopping all day.

She laughed. He was so unpredictable. "Oh, Suede, you amaze me. The adventures you could tell me I'm sure. And yet you always want to hear about Wolfe City and its ranches and people."

"Because they interest you, my sweet." He kissed the tip of her nose.

"Well, for one thing the dance is definitely set for Thursday week. And I've told everyone you'll be there, that they can meet you." She looked worriedly out of the corner of her eye at him. He was still smiling.

"Good!" he shouted. "I'll be glad to meet your friends. I even have a new black suit to wear and by the way, here's a little doo-dad for my girl to pin on her dancing dress." He reached into a pocket, slowly drawing out a small package.

"Now, Suede, not another expensive present. Every time you come you bring me. . . ."

"Shush, my lady, and put it on."

She pinned the cluster of pearls and garnets to her cotton jacket, shaking her head. "But, if you don't have a regular job and can't settle down yet . . . how?"

"No more money talk, woman. Just wear it. And besides, I work," Suede boasted. But his mouth held a strange tension and he hurried to ask, "What else is new?"

"Oh . . . well, the stage was robbed again and everyone was. . . ."

"I heard about that," he clipped. "They know who did it?"

"I don't think so. There's a man, new in town, who swears he's going to catch the thieves. He's likely to do it too—Lon says he will. He found the wreckage but it seems he was chasing this gang even before he found it."

Suede Carson rose and went to the dresser, idly fingering one of her hair pins in a dish. She couldn't see his face. He said, "Oh? What's so special about another posse man?"

"I don't know, except he is a strong, determined-looking man. Of course he's at a disadvantage with only one arm."

The hair pin dropped from Suede's hand and fell to the floor. He muttered something that sounded like "What's his name."

Stooping to search for the pin Abby answered, "Kane Randlett's his name. I invited him to the dance but I don't think he's the dancing kind."

As she stood up Suede Carson looked into her eyes and she had the crazy feeling he didn't see her. She asked, "You will be there by eight o'clock on Thursday, won't you, Suede?"

"Sure honey, sure." He began to pace. Abby knew his moods. They changed quickly like air before a storm, one moment cool and calm, the next hot and angry. She would never be accustomed to them. They baffled her.

"Suede," she pleaded, "please stay and visit tonight."

He stopped pacing. "Next time, Abby. I've just remembered something I forgot to do. Gotta run. Don't worry, I'll be at the dance . . . but I'll probably see you before then." He kissed her cheek and twirling on high-heeled boots, stepped to the window and leaped across the sill.

Abby went to the window, scanning the yard with bewildered eyes. She looked around the corrals, across the field, back to the barn. She could see neither Suede nor his horse.

She touched the sparkling pin on her shirtwaist with a trembling fingertip. Staring at the empty yard, listening to the afternoon stillness in the gathering dusk, she felt a peculiar sense of uneasiness . . . not unlike fear.

Chapter Eight

A dust devil swirled sultry heat off the plain as the two horses clomped lethargically toward the low hills. Their riders were silent in the energy-sapping afternoon. For an hour Lon Bainbridge and Kane Randlett had ridden across a wasteland, huddled on their saddles like dead men.

Randlett glanced at Lon from under his hat brim. He knew Lon was struggling not to cough. He shook his head at the old man's stubbornness. This trip was not good for a weak heart.

Suddenly the air blew cool. The grey picked up his head and began to trot. Ahead in a shallow valley a grove of cottonwoods lined the bank of a clear stream. Beside it a strip of thick grama grass stretched toward the foothills.

Lon reached the stream first. He plopped down beside the water and pulling off his boots stuck dirty stockinged feet into the cold stream. He sighed and let the two horses have their fill. Then wobbling to his feet he hobbled the horses and began to hunt firewood.

Randlett's pack was heavy. He'd brought provisions for several days. He tugged it off, hunting for skillet and bacon.

"Lon . . ." he began, continuing their argument as he stirred the edge of the hot coals with a long stick. Thick salt bacon sputtered and curled brown in the skillet as he rolled flat bread, getting it ready for the hot grease.

Lon's voice interrupted. "No, boy. I've changed my mind. You meet this Injun friend o' yours alone. I'd jus be in the way. I'll hunt fer tracks east o' here then mosey on back to town and wait out the next stage like Draper says."

Although he'd been arguing about it, Randlett was actually relieved Lon decided not to continue. He didn't want leaving Lon out of this to be on his conscience a second time. And Lon was right about Stalking Deer being easier to find if he was alone.

"Round up someone to help you then," Randlett demanded. "One man can't handle that pass."

Lon "hurrumped". "That crew won't strike agin this soon, boy. Noways, not in the same spot."

Randlett heaped bread and bacon on tin plates and opened a can of beans he'd stuck in the hot coals. "Supper," he announced and they ate in weary silence.

Randlett knew Lon better than to keep insisting he posse extra men to help him. Lon was fiercely independent and one rejection was enough. So, he let the matter drop. But he didn't like it. Hot anger washed over him as he thought of Sheriff Draper and his "citified" ideas.

Lon poured boiling hot coffee into their cups. Propped against saddles, they enjoyed the sunset. The grass was rich and thick and they'd sleep well.

After three cups of hot coffee that, "Sure as shootin' restored his bones back to pleasantness," Lon dribbled a ragged stream of tobacco onto yellow paper. Sliding a pointed tongue carefully down one side he looked over at Randlett, deliberately eyed his missing arm and asked, "Boy, one thing always bothered me and I reckon we never talked on it. I know Leek Fetty did thet . . . but why? He trying to kill you and miss?"

Randlett answered quickly. "He didn't miss, Lon. Fetty was not trying to kill me. That idea must have come to him later . . . to gun down the last survivor with his shotgun."

"What then?"

"Fetty wanted me to drop something I had in my hand."

The match burned Lon's finger and he dropped it before the cigarette caught. "That devil! Why boy? What was his notion?"

Randlett eased back against his saddle, settling into a comfortable position. "I told you we had jewels and money with us. Somehow Fetty knew it. Probably by spying on us at the last camp ground . . . we had servants who were free to talk.

"Anyway word leaked out at the stops on the trail we had some riches. When Fetty came in on us and couldn't find any of the jewels or much of the money he went wild, tearing up our packings, still never finding them."

Randlett hesitated. Throughout the years he had tried not to think about the attack and now the exact happenings were vague and distant in his memory. He struggled to recall them. "Pa and me were behind the main wagon when my mother was shot. I tried to run out . . . to fight." He smiled at the memory of his childish bravery. "I had an old paring knife. . . .

"But, Pa stopped me. He grabbed me and whirled me round to face him, talking low and fast about the jewels we had. He pulled the big ring he always wore off his finger . . . he was talking and pushing it into my hand when Fetty roared around the wagon on that dammed black and white horse."

Lon was silent. Randlett threw a pebble at the dying embers. The heat was too much and he turned to his side, resting on his elbow. "Fetty saw what Pa did and he began demanding the ring. Pa shook his head at me shouting, No! Then Pa ran at the horse, trying to jump Fetty. One of the raiders shot him with a six-gun."

Randlett sat up, peering into the darkness surrounding the camp. The next few moments of the tale tried to crowd into his brain and he squinted, wanting to deny their entry. It was not good to remember. But Lon deserved to know.

"Fetty yelled for me to drop the ring and being invincible . . . and not too bright . . . I clenched my fist tighter.

"So, he leveled that beautiful, silver-scrolled shotgun at my arm and let go. The ring rolled away I suppose because I remember one of his men was sent to fetch it. Then Fetty picked up Simon and took off."

Lon coughed, then lit his forgotten cigarette with a hot coal he picked up between two sticks.

Randlett added, "The last thing I remember was Simon screaming. Imagine! Then I guess I passed out 'cause the next thing I knew I was awake to the face and smell and feel of Sun Woman in the Big Lodge."

"Your Cheyenne step-ma," Lon added.

"Yea."

Deputy Bainbridge plopped another log on the coals and asked, "Kane, where were those jewels. You know?"

"No, Lon. I have no idea what happened to them.

Maybe Pa was trying to tell me where they were but I can't recall even the words he said. So, they're lost . . . or buried in my memory. Same thing."

"And Leek Fetty," Lon concluded, "still has that ring."

"Yes, I suppose so."

"And he still has his rotten fangs in young Simon."

Randlett nodded.

Before dawn Randlett was up stoking the coals. He listened with a smile to the honking snores of his sleeping friend. He thought how familiar it sounded even though it had been seven years since they'd spread camp together.

Ten years in all . . . ten years of waiting for a sign of Fetty or Simon. Years misplaced and frustrated that left him as helpless as a stag with locked horns. Now luck, or Fetty's own greed, had changed it and Randlett now had the opportunity to take up where he'd left off . . . to answer Simon's call for help.

Lord, he hoped Simon could hold out. The boy had gumption but he'd need every bit of it and then some if it came to a fight.

Randlett dumped the water out of his canteen, poured last night's coffee on the ground, then went to the stream.

"You still half Injun, ain't you, boy?" Lon remarked, sitting up on his bedroll. Randlett brought the refilled coffee pot to the fire, set it down, his eyebrows arching in acceptance of the fact. Lon added, "No Cheyenne will drink water that's stood all night. That's what you said?"

"Yes. They believe water left sitting in a vessel overnight is dead water. They won't drink it. Guess I do have some of those feelings and habits left," Randlett admitted. "Those were impressionable years for me, Lon. After all, those people saved my life. They became my family."

Lon took the coffee pot and dumped a cup of grounds into it and set in squarely onto red hot coals. "Then you tell that no-count half-brother, Stalking Deer, to do one decent thing in his life and help us git past them Blackfoot."

Randlett said, "I'll ask."

"Way I hear tell it," Lon scowled, "you're a better son than he ever was. You been near 'bout supplyin' that whole ragged Cheyenne camp with grub for the last five years even though you done left 'em long ago."

Lon wagged his head in disgust. "You been doin' what that long-haired rapscallion should been doin' stead o' raisin' Cain on white settlements and gettin' drunk on stolen whiskey. The way I see it he owes you."

"I'm afraid that's not the way Stalking Deer sees it. He and I have always been rivals. He couldn't accept the fact that I did not want to 'take honor' from him. I didn't mean to . . . but things happened to turn it that way. I got lucky and shot a grizzly once. Those claws hang on my spirit shield proclaiming my bravery and telling the world I have power over the beast.

"That could have been Stalking Deer's coup."

Randlett took a sip of the boiling coffee and quickly spat it out. "Darn, Lon, why you think this cools a body off I'll never know." He dumped out the coffee and picked up a can of peaches. He peeled back the top, stuck his knife blade into one and slurped it whole into his blistered mouth.

"And of course there's Magpie," Randlett said after a while. "Stalking Deer thinks I'm going to take her."

"You mean as a squaw wife?" Lon queried. "Well, are you?"

Randlett was silent as he studied the faint, far away hazy shapes of the Buffalo Hollow Hills where the Cheyenne camp lay. Finally he said, "Always had a feeling I would . . . till now. I don't know, Lon."

Something had been bothering him these last few days when he thought of Magpie. Was he finally realizing it was time for him to do the noble thing and clear out . . . get away from her life entirely so that Stalking Deer could claim her? If he thought Magpie could love her cousin, he would. But Randlett feared she wouldn't change. Somehow Magpie had set her heart on the one-armed white boy her family had rescued. And Randlett had always planned to come back someday and take her for his own. Someday ought to be now, he reasoned.

Rising, he packed the empty peach can into his grub sack . . . the women of the camp cut them into bracelets . . . , threw his saddle onto the grey and telling Lon in a falsely hearty voice, "See you in four days in Wolfe City," he mounted in one easy swing.

Lon waved, his mouth full of coffee, his fourth cup of the morning since it would be another hot day.

Chapter Nine

Randlett pointed the gelding toward the north, toward the sprawling rugged canyon area of the Buffalo Hollow Hills. He pushed at a fast clip through the morning hours. At the high point of the sun he had reached Bitter Weed Divide, a stretch of prairie covered with the bitter tasting weeds that marked the beginning of Indian territory. Not government decreed territory rightly claimed by any tribe, but land made sacrosanct by the fact that scalps were taken and white men's camps raided here.

But the Divide was a breathing space where neither white nor red settled. Beyond it, myriad canyons and arroyos and mountain ridges swallowed the bands and villages of Indians. Indians torn from their main branches and converted into frightened, dangerous remnants of their once strong tribes.

Blackfeet, long ago come down from their more northern homeland, had nested in these hills and fought and raided and lived for a generation, keeping for themselves a fertile bit of Pine Mesa in the Fox Tail Mountains.

Randlett's destination was east of Pine Mesa but across the Bitter Weed. Along the northern edge of the Divide he rode for another six or seven miles. The land was sand and fine gravel but in another hour he entered a deep coulee and followed its course into woods. Here he found tracks of ponies and evidence of a Cheyenne camp. But it had been deserted months ago.

He watered the grey, resting in the scrub oaks on a hill. Then he picked up a faint trail leading west.

Late afternoon found him checking on a familiar shady sink under the lee of a short red rock formation. He saw other evidence of his people and pushed on northeast toward the river.

The caw of scissor tails swooping over the grassy knoll that bled into the banks of the Yellow Cat greeted his ears. He breathed thirstily of this lusty damp air, spurring the grey over the rise. At the crest he stood high in the stirrups scanning the valley that stretched to the left of the river canyon. His eyes strained and he was about to leave when he saw what he was searching for . . . a thin, faintly curling stream of smoke deep in the park. The Cheyenne camp.

Randlett rained over the hillock and down into the slope of the river then eagerly into the swift cool water. Horse and rider took their fill of the cold mountain stream.

That old coffee guzzling deputy ought to see *this*, Randlett thought. This water could quench the thirst and cool the blood of *any* man.

He dismounted and began scrutinizing the sand along the bank. He stooped, ran a finger over the dried edges of several dainty hoof prints. He grinned and led the grey up the ravine into a thick copse of pinon pine. Here he left the horse with reins up, and stepping silently, was soon out of sight.

His soft skin-boots made no noise on the thickly matted forest floor. His body, skimming through brush or under trees made no sound to rouse bird or beast. Within five minutes he was seated in a spot camouflaged by dense green leaves. He was downwind from the trail which lay ten feet in front of him.

He waited, scarcely breathing. No thoughts came to his mind. He was adrift. Blank. Primed to act but with no mental consciousness.

A scurrying sound in the leaves caught his attention but it was a small feeding animal and he drifted back in quietness.

The sun bent low over the tops of the pines. No breeze stirred. His head lined up with the trail did not move when the deer appeared. Neither did his eye.

A bluejay squawked but the buck smelled the river and steadily put one hoof before another. He stopped to nip at the tender leaves of a chokecherry bush.

Now he was in clear view directly on the path not ten feet from Randlett. He hesitated only long enough to salute the startled, guileless brown eyes before he lifted the forty-four and fired.

Instantly he curled his fingers around his lips and sent a piercing call for the grey. He then proceeded to tie the front and back legs of the buck, using his foot and his mouth to help the agile hand. He looped one end of another rope over the antlers and threw the other end over a low limb.

As soon as the grey had sniffed his satisfaction at the warm body, Randlett hooked the end of the rope around the saddle horn and clicked his tongue. The grey backed slowly, raising the carcass until it swayed higher than his rump.

Holding it steady, Randlett gutted the hot animal with a long clean slice down the belly. Then swirling the rope around a stump to hold the buck suspended, he let go the loop from off the horn and edged the grey back under the deer. Now he lowered the limp animal onto the fidgety grey and tied it down.

On foot, Randlett led the way out of woods toward the smoke in the valley.

He walked into the edge of the park where he stopped to watch the movements of three women as they dug for roots. Quickly he glanced around until his eye rested on a huge boulder protruding from a swell in the ground on his right. He dropped reins and without a sound ran to the rear side of the rock.

In one swift move he grabbed the small brown leg dangling over the edge and he and the boy fell and tumbled and rolled down the side of the embankment.

Randlett sat astride the wriggling form, pinning both thrashing arms with his one. Wild fear changed to a startled stare as the boy recognized his captor. He smiled a broad happy grin. "Man Alone!" he cried. "You have returned."

"And you, Turtle Boy, are a sentinel to be wished upon the enemy."

The reprimand did not affect the boy. He ran to gather the reins of the grey and lead him proudly into camp.

"Your brother is growing," Randlett spoke to a woman who came toward him. She was more than a head shorter than he and she wore a long tight dress with a square-cut neck that could not hold back the swelling fullness of her figure. Her eyes locked onto Randlett and he could see the happiness and hunger in their darkness. No, he thought, Magpie will not change. He put out his hand and touched the smooth white bone that pierced one ear.

She fell into step beside him.

"You make the lodge of your Mother dwell in happiness today, Man Alone. She grieves for you when you are not here."

"I'm sorry, Magpie, but my spirit calls me to go this way. You know it . . . you have always understood why I cannot remain as a provider in the lodge of my second father."

"Yes," she replied flatly.

"I must work in the white man's world if I am ever to find my brother. And Magpie, I believe I am nearer than ever before." His voice was steel.

She stopped, looking at him not as an unmarried virgin in the camp of her father, but as a restless and eager woman caught between the stable world of her people and the precious glimpse of another, more exciting world which might be hers. "You have signs?"

"Good ones. But I need the help of Stalking Deer."

Magpie moved her head sadly from side to side and Randlett smelled the heavy scent of bear grease on her hair. Not enticing like the odor of jasmine . . . but a smell of strength and nature.

"Stalking Deer has not been here for many moons," she told him. "And you may not receive his help if you find him. He still holds bitterness for you."

"Because he loves you, magpie. You know that." Randlett needed her to understand, to realize she was Cheyenne first, bound by conscience to keep the old ways and she had been promised to Stalking Deer from childhood.

She stiffened. "But he shows no honor to spend his days drinking and fighting . . . I cannot accept that."

"He'll change, Magpie. He is still the same brave,

happy soul we both know. Perhaps he merely needs your promise."

"No, Kane Randlett," she spat harshly, "You are wrong. He must be a man *before* he can have my promise." She turned away and left him.

The women were gathered in front of the lodge of Sun Woman. The children laughed and played and drew lots for the precious ears of the buck. Three girls watched the older women as they strung, cut and skinned the animal. Sun Woman squatted flat-footed before her fire. She was already preparing the choice bits of liver and heart for the white warrior . . . her son.

She rose when he approached. "My son," she said with tears in her old eyes, and went into her tent to greet him with talk.

She immediately saw the bullet hole in his hat and began repairing it. "You fight often, Man Alone?"

Seeing her anguish he said, "I know it hurts you, my mother, that I go into the white world and fight. But I have been searching for my brother and I have found sign, and now I must stop the man who took him."

The flap of the lodge was raised and Walks Around entered. Despite the years which showed in his face in crisscrossing grooves like lines on a map, Sun Woman's man held his stoop-shouldered figure with grace.

Walks Around was only part of his name. In Cheyenne he was "He Walks Around With The Weight of The World On His Shoulders." This came to be his name during the last thirty years when he spent his time and heart and youth trying to keep peace.

He greeted Randlett with a hug, calling for a feast in honor of Man Alone who had brought food and gifts and the strengthening spirit of the Maijun.

During the ceremonial meal Randlett gave out his

gifts. Magpie accepted a necklace of golden beads. Sun Woman sat reverently all evening in the hot air, her new wool shawl wrapped snugly around her shoulders.

Later, near dawn when the women and children had gone to bed and most of the men lay near the dying fires, Randlett and Walks Around smoked together in the lodge.

"Stalking Deer comes only when he needs to refill his belly or to see his cousin." Walks Around puffed on the long pipe.

"I must talk with him," Randlett said. "He knows the Blood who live in the Fox Tails. I need him to exchange a passage for me."

"Little Crooked Feather has been to Stalking Deer's camp in the hills. It is only one of many camps of the great 'fighting man'." Walks Around's voice was full of disgust but his face was shadowed by the hurt and dishonor his son had heaped upon him. "And he cannot always be found there. But Crooked Feather will show you this place."

At daybreak Randlett rolled onto a bed of pine boughs and slept. Midafternoon he rose and strolled to the stream to wash. The cold water stung him awake and he shaved and donned a new shirt.

Then he went to say good-bye to Sun Woman. As he left the lodge, Magpie appeared. She handed him a parcel of pemmican. "I was angry for no cause, Man Alone," she said. "I ask it to be forgotten."

Randlett smiled. "It is forgotten. But listen to me as a faithful friend, Magpie. You know the heart of Stalking Deer. You know his trouble is like the wildness of the hurt wolf, something that will soon leave when he is healed. But he is the same Tom Stalking Deer we both know. Remember how he wove belts for you from the willow flowers? And remember how he looked for you first when we returned from a hunt? He loves you, Magpie."

Magpie watched a small lizard dart to the shade of a mullein plant. She said nothing but her breast rose and fell with her breathing.

"Stalking Deer will go into the Fox Tails with me, Magpie, and lead me to my brother. You must think on that so that you may treat him with honor."

Randlett had no idea why he wanted her to believe in Stalking Deer . . . to accept his love. Had he himself already decided not to claim her? The pulse of a strong-willed woman beat in her heart. He could ask her to wait for him and she would. He could ask her to leave her people and go with him and she would.

But he mounted the grey and joined young Crooked Feather.

Chapter Ten

Crooked Feather led through tight, narrow wedges along the winding path. Sharp, spiked slivers of rock jutted out from the sides of the canyon walls. It was a forlorn and threatening place. A place to whet the anger and ill temper of anyone daring to call it home.

A shiver coursed up Randlett's spine. If Stalking Deer chose to live here then the young Indian had a desperate need to feed his anger.

Crooked Feather pointed across a crack in the rock floor, one too wide for his pony to jump. "Cross here." He gestured up the slope. "Behind the high wall is the fire of your brother. He keeps his horse in a bush-fence where there is water."

"You were brave to show me the way, Crooked Feather. Return to camp before the sun falls."

Randlett watched the boy ride for home, then touching heels to the grey he lunged across the broken rock. The gelding's flanks were lathered white and foam flecked his lips. This is hellish going for man *or* horse, Randlett thought angrily.

On the other side of the cut he dismounted and began to search for signs of the Indian. They were on a slate ledge and stepping carefully, he led the horse around the mountain wall.

Fifty yards below in a natural enclosure of buckbrush and thistle, Randlett saw a small seep of water, one of those natural catches where rain settled, or water flowed from mountain cracks.

He went to the tiny cup of water and refilled his canteen. Then he let the gelding suck up the remains. Crooked Feather was right. A horse had been kept here. But many days ago, the spoor were dry.

Pulling saddle and bridle, Randlett poured a small sack of oats onto hard rock for the grey to eat.

Pushing his sweat-stained hat off his forehead he let his gaze travel in a circle over the surroundings. He sensed he was alone. He climbed under a high ridge of rock that hung over the canyon floor. In the large open cave it formed were remains of a fire. He kicked at the charred coals. Weeks old, he guessed.

Besides the fire, there was nothing to indicate a man ever slept under the ledge. No cigarette butts, no discarded gun shells, no chewed-on bones, no imprints of a body or boot. Randlett shook his head. Even here Stalking Deer had not felt safe, he left nothing of himself to claim the place.

Then Randlett's gaze lingered on the soot-stained overhanging roof. Smiling wryly he reached up to touch the lines and patterns etched with a knife. Stalking Deer could never resist drawing designs with any tool on any surface. These designs were unfinished, not like his usual perfect completions that swirled and locked together in mysterious beauty. These told Randlett that Stalking Deer had made them unconsciously, then quit, realizing he might be leaving a sign of himself.

Out from the enclosure, Randlett climbed to a slim rock tower where he sat the rest of the day. He chewed the pemmican Magpie had given him and watched. He saw no one.

When early darkness creeped onto the canyon floor, Randlett built a fire from the thick underlimbs and roots of the dried buckbrush. He boiled coffee and fried a potato in bacon grease. Sopping up the grease with a hard biscuit, he sat uneasily on his heels. Snakes often came out at night toward heat . . . such as a fire . . . or a human body.

The next day he saw no sign of Stalking Deer. He was up early and after a cup of leftover coffee he went to the water hole. Several gallons had seeped into the cup during the night and he drank deeply before refilling his canteen.

Off and on during the day he sat on the tower peek or scouted about in a circle, trying to pick up the Indian's trail. He found nothing.

At the end of the second day Randlett decided he had met another blank wall. The grey needed grass, and as old father had said, Stalking Deer had many homes.

He was pulling dry brush from the corral for his evening fire when the racking ping of a bullet struck rock a foot from his head. Randlett whirled, crouching, at the same instant drawing his pistol.

A second rifle shot zinged into the gravel at his feet. He flipped into a roll, coming up half crawling, half running to the safety of the tower. On the other side he hunkered against the talus wall.

A crow cawed, then there was hot silence.

He was hot himself, his breath coming in long gasps. Who was out there? Was it Stalking Deer?

A rockslide drew his attention to the rise in front of him. In one swift move his gun was levelled and he pulled his knees up, ready to leap. His face was flushed and salty sweat dripped into his eyes.

His eye fastened toward the top of the rockslide, Randlett slowly began to rise. As he stood up, a man jumped cat-cleaver onto the floor not twenty feet in front of him.

The Indian wore nothing but a breechclout and short moccasins. A red flannel strip was tied around his head, securing the long straight hair that hung to his shoulders. He was a stocky man—like his father—and tough-skinned as any wild animal living in these harsh surroundings had to be. He held a rifle pointed at Randlett's chest.

The muscles on Randlett's chest quivered but he lowered the Colt. "I seek the man I know as Stalking Deer," he said firmly. "A man of generosity who shared his home with me when I was wounded and lost . . . a man who was proud when he taught me useful ways so that I might survive in his land."

A smile had started on Randlett's lips. But it froze as he looked into Stalking Deer's eyes. The black orbs glittered with hate that Randlett knew was fueled by pride and hurt.

The Indian's rifle boomed and the slug sliced a trail along Randlett's cheek. He flinched, then gritted his teeth and spoke with slow deliberation from deep within his guts, "The man Stalking Deer does not shoot his brother."

Another bullet tore a hole in Randlett's collar, sending a stream of blood running down his neck.

Trembling, Randlett put his wrist to his mouth. His teeth sank into the cuff of his shirt-sleeve and as he drew his arm away he pulled back the sleeve, leaving his arm bare. He turned the exposed inner arm toward Stalking Deer who stood paralyzed, eyes hooded, glaring at it.

Randlett kept his arm facing the Indian. As he watched, Stalking Deer stared at the line of death-scars running the length of the arm. The scars matched those coursing down his own right arm. Cuts the two brothers had once made on themselves at the death of a friend.

Stalking Deer's teeth ground together. Randlett could see those dark eyes softening, turning away. A guttural choking sound came from the war-painted chest of his red brother and he lowered the rifle.

They went to the open cave and sat cross-legged beside the dead fire. Randlett gave Stalking Deer some jerked meat and biscuits. While the Indian ate Randlett told him about Simon and Fetty's gang raiding again. Stalking Deer grunted that he knew it already.

After eating, Stalking Deer wiped his hands on his breechclout and said, "I am Tom. I am Tom Stalking Deer."

Randlett squinted. Then trying not to grin he shook his head. "Yes," he said, "You are Tom Stalking Deer."

Stalking Deer had always wanted to be called by the American name, Tom. He had made a big to-do about it but no one had paid attention. It seemed useless at the time and Randlett had never thought about it again. Now he realized it represented Stalking Deer's freedom, his breaking away and the recognition of his manhood in the real world.

Randlett put his hand on the wound on his neck. It still bled and it stung like a million ants. He said, "I believe Simon is being held captive in the Fox Tails, maybe on the Tepee. I intend to find him but I need your help, St . . . Tom Stalking Deer, to get past the Blood."

Stalking Deer was silent, his arms folded across his knees, his eyes wary. Finally he spoke. "The Blood who live beyond the Fox Tails are not honorable men. The young braves do as they please. Their chief is old and stupid. He wears a secret name that changes with the moon. No one can enter his tent without his name on their tongue."

Randlett frowned. "What is his name now? Do you know?"

Stalking Deer rose and began to pace the cave. Randlett knew this hot-headed Indian brother was still not pleased to be talking with him. He could feel the anger rising in Stalking Deer's voice as he said, "I have heard his new name is Red Vest. He took such a prize from a trader and he is never without it. He desires such white men's garments. He is a fool."

Randlett said softly, "But still he is chief and he could get his people to let me pass if you go with me. I have heard it said that all red men know you and do not want you for an enemy."

Stalking Deer nodded to the truth of that, then said with a cunning grin, "Perhaps if Tom Stalking Deer had reason to do such a thing . . . ?"

Randlett sighed. He knew what Stalking Deer wanted. He wanted Randlett to give in . . . to go away and leave the territory so that Magpie would forget him. Well, Randlett thought, maybe now I can reassure him. If he'll accept what I say.

"I have been to see your cousin and she waits for you to come back with honor. If you take me through the Blo. . . ."

"No! Magpie does not wait for Tom Stalking Deer.

She waits for Man Alone to give ponies to her father. She waits for you! It is for the safety of Kane Randlett that she would have me lead you into the Fox Tails."

The Indian spat at Randlett's feet and turning, disappeared into the rocks.

Chapter Eleven

Randlett left the dry, desolate mountain a disappointed man. But he was a natural hunter and he already had an idea he wanted to talk over with Lon that might be another way through or around the Blackfeet.

As he hit the end of Main Street he knew something was wrong. Stores were closed. Hack's barber shop was locked tight. No buggies were tied at the rails along the dusty street.

A cold finger touched the back of his neck when he turned the corner. A cluster of people stood together on top of the cemetery hill. The cracked alto voice of an elderly lady peeled out, "I'll never cross Jordan alone. . . ."

With a dry throat Randlett rode to the foot of the hill. He stopped and waited for the group of mourners to break up. Sheriff Draper was talking to several men and Randlett recognized Abby and Pat McMillan. When they saw him they started toward him.

Abby wore a black dress, a veil covering her hair.

Even through the heavy veil Randlett could see the girl's eyes were red, her features haggard and drawn.

Pat McMillan was poker-faced and Abby clung to his arm as if she were drunk.

"He tried, Mr. Randlett. . . ." she cuttingly said as they drew near. She fought for control, her voice choked with emotion. Then gathering herself up she spat, "Lon should never have been allowed to go alone on such an 'escort' mission. He was too old and sick to be responsible for stopping that gang!"

Pat McMillan put his hat on and added, "Lon Bainbridge was shot, Randlett . . . on that escort trip. The Fetty bunch hit at the pass and Lon was killed along with those on the stage."

The strength left Randlett's legs. So that he wouldn't collapse he began to move, lumbering up the hill. In a trance he passed the other mourners.

Someone had sprinkled flower petals over a hump of newly turned earth. As Randlett stared at it his eyes clouded over and a sob broke from his chest. "You evil, son of a . . ." he muttered. "I'll get you, Leek Fetty, if it's the last thing I do on earth."

Leaning against the pull of the earth, rooted and swaying like a tree, Randlett stood with his hand crushing the brim of his hat. He stood for an hour and did not know it.

When he walked down the hill his mind was clear. He would go after this killer alone. He would probably be killed himself, but that didn't matter. He asked only that he be allowed to put the final bullet into that cursed man Fetty.

First, he needed information.

Will Draper was sitting at his desk staring at the pencil he held between two nervous fingers. The twitching stopped when Randlett came in. "Have a seat. Have a seat," he said.

Randlett thought the sheriff seemed unsure of himself and he demanded, "What are you going to do, Draper?"

"I . . . ah." One hand ran to the back of his neck and he thumped the pencil on the desk. Taking a breath he said, "It was just rotten luck, Randlett. Bainbridge shouldn't have been shot. He was following off the road and had plenty time to get away."

"Get away!" Randlett couldn't believe it. "Lon was a lawman, Draper. He was responsible. He wouldn't get away!"

"Yes, well, I'm sorry for your sake. I know how much you counted on him. But I have things turning, Randlett. I closed off the pass road so that we could study the tracks . . . I believe they are quite clear . . . though I haven't yet gotten anyone . . . with the funeral and all. . . . But . . . but, I've sent word to Conger City with a description of those three we know about. They'll make wanted posters and we can send these out to every town within a radius of one hundred miles.

"And by the way," he continued, "I've been told you shot that Mexican the gambler mentioned. Is it true? If so, I'll need a report."

Randlett closed his burning eyelids. "Make your own report, I don't have time." He stood up and asked, "Was there any money on that stage, Draper?"

The sheriff's face sagged. "Well, yes, some."

"How much?"

"That's government business. . . ."

Randlett slapped an iron fist on the desk. A thunderous scowl wrinkled his forehead. "How much, Draper?"

"Ten thousand."

"Ten thou. . . . I thought you assured us this was a no-hit proposition."

"We have no idea how they knew about it, Randlett. All the men that I . . . who knew . . . swear they told no one."

"All the men. How many did you tell about the money, Draper?"

Ignoring the question, the sheriff opened a drawer. "Here is Deputy Bainbridge's gun, Randlett. You may have it since he had no next of kin."

Randlett took the pistol, broke it, counted the spent cartridges. Two live bullets remained.

"Lon got in some shots," Draper explained. "But not the one that counted it seems. You see, he was found behind a rock. He had fired upon the gang but for some reason he let that Fetty ride right up and . . . and shoot him."

Randlett flared, gulping a wave of hot rage about to overwhelm him. "Then Lon was shotgunned?"

"Yes, Randlett."

Randlett swore and walked out of the office.

The grey was tired but Randlett leaped into the saddle and dug in his heels. He headed for the pass. Two days had passed since the hold-up but the weather had been calm, no rain, no wind. And Draper at least had done one good thing in closing the road. He just might get some clear tracks.

He was right. The soft sand on the curve before the chasm had left a story in hoof prints . . . both man and horse. For a long sweat-drenching hour Randlett studied them. He carefully placed each different hoof print into his mind, noting the curve, chip, size, depth, characteristic flip or dance or jiggle each horse made.

There had been five horses. Randlett wiped his face with his handkerchief. Morrales was dead and if the Mexican was correct about seeing six riders, then that would mean Simon was with this skirmish. Perhaps on that smaller horse that seemed to stay near the edge of the fray? Pray yes, Randlett thought.

He had waited to study the area where Lon had been shot. Now taking a deep breath he walked closer, toward the front of the huge boulder where that grand Appaloosa would have danced. The picture was too plain. Only one horse came this close to the rock. Just as he thought, these were the prints of the largest, heaviest horse . . . one larger than any of the others. It reared once, dropped, then bounded within ten feet of the rock.

Randlett bent near the prints. The right rear hoof had a habit of slewing out and back. Randlett measured it, touched it, burned the look of it into his mind. Never again would he see this print and not know it.

When he stood up he realized how close the horse had come to the edge of Lon's cover. Lon had had two remaining shots . . . why hadn't he fired? Was he wounded? No, that shotgun blast had been his only wound.

Randlett frowned. Oh, Lon, he wondered, what happened . . . why didn't you shoot?

The tracks of the bushwhackers as they gathered at the road's edge pointed north toward the Fox Tails. Randlett let the gelding set his own pace, stopping or slowing enough to keep the tracks in sight.

An hour later, at a low place near the Yellow Cat, the prints became a crazy mixture. They criss-crossed one another . . . as if the men riding were arguing about which direction to take.

Randlett noticed four of them finally pulled up the far

bank and continued toward the Tails. But one, and it was not the Appaloosa, headed east.

One of the men was going somewhere else. Who? And for what reason? Perhaps to put the money in a safer place? But that didn't fit with what he believed about Leek Fetty. That man would not let ten thousand dollars leave his side.

I can always go on to the hills, Randlett decided. I'll follow this lone rider. One will be easier to confront than the whole bunch. Randlett's stomach tightened at the thought of getting his hands on one of these killers.

The trail of the lone horse led through a dry rocky plain. Randlett lost it twice before the tracks ambled into grazing land and he had to spend time picking them up again. The grass on the grazing meadow was green and deep and had been pushed down by a single horse. Randlett was not surprised to see sleek red longhorns scattered over the hills. He could see no brands.

When the sun began to burn red Randlett reined up in timber beside the southern tip of the Yellow Cat. The bandit had rested at the river. He had eaten near the water's edge and filled his canteen . . . boot marks on the muddy bank showed plainly.

As Randlett stooped to drink, a blur of color caught his eye. Near the edge of the bank, stuffed among the cattails, was a piece of cloth. Curious, he pulled it out and held it up. It was a man's shirt. It was a medium sized garment, nearly new, but there was a tear under the right arm and along the edges was a brown circle. Randlett recognized it as dried blood. And the tear was a bullet hole.

Randlett's breathing speeded up. They had come mighty close to getting another of the gang. Lon had bit this one for sure.

But where was he headed? A doctor maybe? Yet from the small amount of blood he could tell the wound was not severe.

Randlett followed at a faster pace.

Another thirty minutes and he came onto a bunch of cattle with the Double M brand. Pat McMillan's spread. And the tracks were still clear, as if the rider did not care if he were followed.

When Randlett pulled around a back corral near a barn he rode up to the fence where a cowboy was working a cutting horse. The man was sweaty and hot but he spoke in a light-hearted friendly tone. "Lookin' fer a job? If'n y'ar, you can shure take my place come daylight. Never rode such a meanun."

"Don't need a job but I do need some information," Randlett said. "Day before yesterday a man . . . a friend of mine . . . rode in from this way. You remember seeing him?"

The cowboy yanked the rope on the horse's halter and shook his head. "Not I recall and I'm here on Mondays. As I remember Miss McMillan's sweetie come acourtin' agin that day and he often times rides in from that northwest pasture—same as you jus done."

"You saw him ride in that day?"

"Naw. Only saw them together after he come in. Matter of fact they're off ridin' right now. Way I figure it, he's scared of her pa. Don't know why unlessen he plans some shenanigans. Then he better look out."

"So no stranger has been around here lately?"

"Sorry."

Randlett leaned on the corral fence as the cowboy led the bronc away. He needed to think. He knew trailing. He was not wrong about these tracks leading straight to this ranch. That left only one out. Abby McMillan's sweetie must be one of the gang.

And . . . a hard lump stuck in Randlett's throat at the thought . . . if that were true it could mean the man she knew as Suede Carson was really Simon.

That couldn't be, he muttered, slinging his head in disbelief. Because in that case Simon was free to leave the gang.

Except, he told himself, if Simon were being blackmailed somehow. Damn! What a situation.

Chapter Twelve

Randlett strode over to the open barn and looked in. The cowboy said Abby was out with her feller right now. What a chance, he thought.

Before he could decide where to wait, a horse and rider galloped around the corner and Abby McMillan reined up in front of him. "Mr. Randlett," she cried, "what are you doing at the Double M?"

Grabbing the bit strap of the fidgety mare Randlett said, "I'd like to talk to you, Miss McMillan."

She leaped off, then led the mare into the open barn. "Very well, talk."

"Where've you been?"

"Wh . . . why that's rather impertinent, Mr. Randlett, and quite none of your business." She threw him a surly look as she jerked at the cinch.

Randlett hadn't thought how his request would sound. He ran anxious fingers through his hair. He gazed at her slim figure, noticing she was hot and evidently tired. Seeing her fumbling efforts with the unsaddling, he moved up to take charge.

Abby seemed relieved. Untying her hat she slipped it off and began to fan with it. The shade of the barn was cooler than the hot outside air but still it was suffocating. The odors of hay and the dank, rich smell of manure were strong.

"I'm sorry, Miss McMillan," Randlett said. "I guess I'm upset and I can see that you are too. Lon's death was unnecessary. It shouldn't have happened."

Abby McMillan leaned back against the wall, her eyes closed. Glancing up at her, Randlett feared she would faint. She had a frighteningly haggard appearance. Dark circles underlined her pale-lidded eyes.

"The fact is," he went on, "I was wondering if you'd been riding with your friend. Didn't you say his name was Suede Carson?"

Randlett hooked the bridle on the nail that was over her head to his left. As he reached for it her upturned face, resting against the barn wall, was only inches from his own. He could see the throbbing pulse in the hollow of her throat. That faint aroma of jasmine, mingling with the warm heat of her body rose up to meet him. His chest tightened.

Letting out a long, easy breath he stepped back and began uncinching the saddle.

Abby answered his question while her eyes remained closed. "Yes," she said in a flat, exhausted voice, "his name is Suede Carson and I was riding with him." Suddenly her eyes flew open and she asked, "How did you know?"

Randlett didn't answer but asked, "Has your father told you anything about who I am—why I'm after Fetty?"

Her face softened, she looked steadily at him, compassion shading her green eyes. "Yes, he has. And I'm sorry about your brother."

"Then you know that I believe Simon is being held somehow . . . or forced to ride with the gang in these raids."

"I . . . I guess so," she said, interested despite herself.

Randlett yanked off the saddle and hefted it over the stall wall. "I went back to the sight of the hold-up this morning, Miss McMillan, and trailed the bushwhackers out onto the prairie. Their trail headed toward the Fox Tails."

She waited, studying the sheer energy of his movements as he easily poured a bucket of grain and edged the mare into the stall. His missing arm did not seem to deter him in anything.

"Some two miles from the hold-up one of the riders split, headed out on his own. I trailed him here."

She scowled, not understanding. "I assure you we've not had a visit by any such. . . ."

"On the day of the robbery, Miss McMillan, think back. Did someone come to the ranch in the late afternoon? Maybe to visit your dad or to see one of the hands?"

"No. I was here all day, I worked in the garden and would have seen any such person. But you're welcome to ask our boys."

"Your hands tell me that your friend Suede Carson visited you late that afternoon." Randlett was sweating under his shirt. He felt a peculiar prickling sensation. His mind did not want to accept the one conclusion all the facts seemed to demand . . . Abby McMillan's sweet-talking fellow and his kid brother who could always wrap Ma and all the other women he ever knew right around his little finger were one and the same."

Randlett asked carefully, "Now Miss McMillan this is mighty important. Did Suede Carson have a wounded arm that day, on Monday, the day of the robbery?"

"No," she cried, anger clouding her eyes. She strode to the open doors then stopped. With a deep scowl on her smooth white forehead she added in a voice so low he could barely hear, "That is, I didn't notice. He came in about six and we went for our usual ride. Dad hadn't gotten back yet from town and of course I hadn't learned about Lon.

"Suede got off his horse I remember and . . . and he looked a little pale so I. . . . Mr. Randlett, what are you implying?"

Bracing himself for the conclusion he said, "I have a strong hunch that your friend Suede Carson . . . may be my brother."

Abby gave a small squeak and put her hand to her mouth. She began to back away. "No, no," she said.

"I don't mean he is one of them. I think he is forced to go with them. Look, you don't know this Fetty . . . he is a demon who gets whatever he wants and he has had his hands on my brother for all his growing up years. Now tell me, where is Suede Carson from? Who are his parents? Where does he work?"

Abby McMillan crumpled onto a bale of hay, her hands rubbing together in her lap. "This is impossible. . . ."

"Listen," Randlett moved to her side. "I believe my brother is held against his will by some threat. I need to find him. To talk to him. To let him know I'm here."

"No. . . ."

"You don't have to believe anything. Just arrange a meeting for me with your friend. That's all I want."

She stiffened, picked up her crop and began nervously hitting her boot. "It couldn't be. Why, he . . . he actually knows of a Kane Randlett who is chasing the Fetty gang. We talked about you."

Randlett wavered. Was he wrong? That lone rider may have only chanced upon the ranch and ridden away. But it was too unlikely. That rider was on a known course. "Does Suede Carson always meet you here, then take you out to do his courting?"

She bristled. "We don't hide, Mr. Randlett, if that's what you mean."

But he never takes you where other people are?"

A glimmer sparked in her eyes at that and she turned to leave. "Oh yes he does. As a matter of fact he's coming to the dance on Thursday. He'll gladly meet you and all of my friends."

Randlett started for his horse then paused. "Miss McMillan?"

"Yes?" she waited condescendingly for one more question.

"But this will be the first time Suede Carson has met any of your friends . . . won't it."

She flushed a deep red and slamming her hat against her skirt, hurried toward the ranch house.

Chapter Thirteen

By mid-day he had picked up the trail of the four outlaws. Under a misty rain the sign was hazy, in some places he guessed at it. But he knew if he kept toward that low-hanging line of blue mountains that lay against the horizon like the fine soft fluff of M'Lady's best fur cape, he would come upon them again.

Randlett wished desperately for two arms. He needed a rifle against these men and one thing he couldn't do was handle a long gun. Without a rifle he'd have to get close. Real close. The same as deer hunting, he told himself. The pistol would have to do.

This trek was a gamble at any rate. If the men had gone through the Fox Tails, past the Blood, and reached their hideout on the Mesa . . . then he'd not find them. But if he knew men, they had stopped to rest, to drink in celebration, maybe even to wait for that lone rider.

When darkness came he had reached the foot of the mountains. The light rain had pelted down all day and he was soaked. Under his tarp he made a fire and fried three strips of deer meat. He ate them rolled up in a dough he wrapped around green sticks and baked. Dried apples finished his meal along with a pot of coffee.

Over the last cup he sat for a long time thinking of Lon. The taste was bitter, and swearing silently, he spat it out.

He entered the foothills the next morning. A line of heavy timber of mixed pine and cedar grew along the base then spread in scattered sections as the land climbed higher. A rushing stream flowed down the largest promontory, feeding the small valleys between the lower ridges.

Signs were long ago washed out but there was a trail. Men and animals always took the easiest path and over time wore a trail that became permanent. The Indians who crossed the Fox Tails and were headed for the Bitter Weed Divide and hence to the free camping grounds beyond, came this way . . . the bandits likely followed this same trail.

Randlett rode with his hand free, close to the forty-four.

Out of the hilly timber the trail cut between two fingers of the mountain. A side-creek of the big Yellow Cat rumbled down the incline washing out a wide sandy bank. Shunning the reeds growing on the edges, Randlett searched the low-sloping banks for hoof prints.

He sat tall, urging the gelding up a steeper bank. A chill wind sent low rolling clouds scudding overhead. He urged the grey up to a point along the bank and the gelding nickered, resisting. At the crest Randlett hunkered into his poncho and pushed for the stand of cedars up ahead.

Pressing his calves, Randlett signalled the grey to stop. A horse was tethered to the right at the edge of a clearing. In the center of the clearing a man crouched beside a fire.

Randlett levelled the forty-four at the man's body, his eye roving the corners of the glade. The man seemed not to notice him and Randlett threw a leg over the grey and eased off.

He walked to the fire.

The man was small, grizzled, with a dirty, grey-streaked beard. He moved in an easy manner but his crinkled rheumy eyes were belligerent as they swiveled onto Randlett. "Coffee in a minute, boy," he said. "No need for that hole blower."

Despite the coontail hat the man wore Randlett was certain he was no trapper. His pack was a simple bedroll.

The ancient poured a cup and handed it to him. "You're Kane Randlett ain't you." Randlett shoved the forty-four into the holster to take the cup. Then setting the cup on a rock he eased back. He glanced quickly around but the rain obscured sight from more than ten feet into the outer mist.

The old man spat a stream of tobacco, wiped his mouth with his sleeve and said, "Heard 'bout you back in Wolfe City."

His muscles tensing, Randlett feared he'd stepped into trouble. "You one of Fetty's?" he asked.

The icy words that came from the old coon were like the warning of a hell-fire preacher. "Best you ride on, son. Fast."

A clap of thunder brought a cold down-pour into the glade and Randlett turned. But not soon enough. Two rifles clicked at the edge of the woods and a voice rang, "Throw it out!"

Randlett blinked into the falling rain at the two outlaws who strode into the firelight. He tossed out his gun.

"Ye should'uv toook the mon's adveese, Mr. Randlett," the big Irishman shook his head in mock sadness.

Randlett answered, "I want to see your boss." He still had no way of knowing what position Simon held with these men . . . but it must be of some import since this old man had challenged him to move on rather than pull a gun.

"The boss only wants you to leave the country, son," the old man put in, giving him one more chance to get out.

The short, bow-legged hombre beside the Irishman kept quiet but Randlett knew his kind. He feared that nervous, steely-eyed hardcase more than the other two combined.

"Sorry ye didna take yer leave whun ye had the chance," red-beard said. "New let's get it over with," he addressed the old man who began to shake his head from side to side.

"We were to scare him off, O'Riley, so we'll have to figure another way." Rain splashed into the coffee cup as the old codger lifted it to his lips, straining it through his matted beard.

The nervous twerp finally spoke. "If the boss wus here he'd use his pumper," he offered and grinned. Randlett could tell he was ready for the showdown. The man built a cigarette with one hand while the other hooked onto a rifle that was taller than he was.

"Shure and since he isn't, you'll oblige him with a mite o' help from yer own big ol' gun, huh, Bugs?" O'Riley teased.

"That's enough, boys," McPherson ordered. It was clear he had the say in the situation. But O'Riley had a bull of a body with a head to match and Randlett knew he'd fight like one.

"Tie him," McPherson said.

"And how do ye tie a mon with but one arm, mind ya?" O'Riley laughed as he strode over to the grey. He lifted the rope and swatted the gelding's rump, sending him off into the pines.

Then the giant, standing a head taller than Randlett, looped the three-quarter inch rope over Randlett's head and pulled his arm to his side with a crushing force that cut the circulation and sent Randlett gasping for breath.

The nervously dancing spitfire had his rifle pointed at Randlett's gut as O'Riley tied his legs and dumped him under a nearby tree. "Ye'll not need yer fine gun this night," O'Riley told his cohort with a wink. "So don't be afeered."

Bugs Harper whirled on his dainty-toed boots and centered his rifle on O'Riley's laughing face. The Irishman dropped his smile. The two stood eye to eye.

"Coffee!" Soda McPherson called. The two bushwhackers slowly turned away but continued to glower at each other. Bugs Harper accepted the hot brew. O'Riley went to a war-bag on the ground and dug out a bottle. The grin back on his swarthy face, he up-ended the flask and downed enough white mule to bring tears to his eyes.

Soon the three robbers were hunched over the spitting fire, grumbling, laughing, swearing oaths of "Git it done, damn it!" into the storm.

Randlett's body ached from the tightness of the ropes and the position he was forced to take. His feet were numb. He shook his head trying to clear his thoughts. Since I didn't leave, he reasoned, they'll find it acceptable to kill me. With that thought he knew what to do.

He began drawing his feet up toward his hand. Then slowly he pulled his arm back and forth within the rope, struggling to loosened it enough so that his hand could touch the top of his right boot.

An hour later the muscles in Randlett's long lean frame quivered. He felt exhausted. He was cold and yet his body was covered with sweat.

The men were quiet. Asleep? Randlett couldn't see. If he were going to get away he'd better do it now. He began to wiggle in earnest, his hand edging inside his boot. His cold, stiff fingers grasped the bone-handled knife of Earnesto Morales and pulling it carefully from the boot he turned it up and began to saw on the ropes around his arm and body. Then the ones on his legs. When the ropes finally parted he called, "Hey!"

When nothing happened he called louder, "Hey!"

Again he called as he hid the two-edged knife under his hip.

O'Riley swaggered up. His red, whiskey-sapped face held a satisfied leer. In his right hand his forty-five swayed back and forth. "They're fahst asleep me friend. They'll not blame me fer havin' to shoot ye tryin' to git away. . . ." A sour smile creased O'Riley's lips as the tip of the gun touched Randlett's chest.

"But first ye'll need a bit o' persuasion. . . ." And the giant's left hand clenched into a fist the size of a cannon ball and he let go with a roundhouse blow aimed at Randlett's jaw. If the man had been sober the blow would have killed Randlett. But O'Riley stumbled as he swung, and Randlett jerked his head to one side in time to receive only a split lip.

"Uggh!" O'Riley grunted as he fell to his knees. The forty-five went off with a boom and Randlett felt a hot sting on his shoulder. "You . . ." he started, then pushing himself from under the heavy beast, he rammed the knife into the Irishman's fat stomach.

O'Riley screamed, fell into the wet leaves, thrashing and crying. Randlett jumped to his feet, nearly fell, but he flipped around, away from the fire. Stumbling, crawling, sliding, he tore through the trees toward the river bank.

He dared not glance up but ran frantically down a bramble-strewn creekbed. He ran with a burning shoulder and a bleeding mouth, his breath coming in harsh gasps.

The gully petered out, and Randlett fell trying to gain the far bank. The bank was muddy and he kept slipping. Finally he clutched a tangle of roots and pulled himself up through a sloping fissure.

He was near the top when the crack of a rifle bullet brought him up sharp. Bugs Harper and the venerable Soda McPherson stood overhead with cocked guns.

Wanting a better aim, Harper stepped to the side, over a rock, and as he moved, the ledge gave way and he plummeted down in a scurry of dirt, needles and wild cursings.

Randlett fell with him, wrenching the rifle from the startled grip of the little man as they crashed together. Bounding to his feet, Randlett swung the gun like a tomahawk. It thudded into Harper's head with such force they were both knocked into the slimy mass of water at the bottom of the gully.

Hot bullets spewed dirty water, missing Randlett's legs by inches. Harper slithered to the left, twisting his body in front of Randlett, halting McPherson's fire.

Snaking free of a dazed Bugs Harper, Randlett broke into the reeds and marsh along the opposite bank. Crouched over, he ran back down the ravine.

Scanning the banks for roots large enough to hold his weight, Randlett listened for the bandits. Their commotion ceased and he imagined them slinking through the timber along the edge of the stream.

A half-dead tree, its roots open and protruding, gave him his ladder. Clawing at the short weeds on the embankment, keeping his body turned so that he could balance, he scurried up and over the ledge, falling with a gasp of pain.

His eyes gazed over the camp. O'Riley's body lay near the firepit, face down. Randlett ran to find his gun. It was lying near one of the packs.

A flurry of cracking branches came from the pines near the creak and Randlett jumped to dodge a crossfire of pinging bullets. He fired once at Harper, then dived behind a group of saplings. A funny, hurt animal sound came to his ears and he peered out to see that his slug had split a dark furrow on Harper's head, creasing his hair.

The cock had stopped in his tracks, dumbfounded. Suddenly swiveling first to the left, then to the right, he peppered the edge of the clearing with a barrage of wild shots.

But Randlett had left the saplings. He was running behind the campfire . . . toward the pines where the grey had been booted.

Slipping around the trees he slid to a halt in a small open meadow. The gelding was standing head high, alert to the sound of gunfire. One sharp whistle and the grey stomped toward Randlett who swiftly yanked himself into the saddle and nudged the grey away from the glade back down toward the river.

Chapter Fourteen

He had never been so tired. As soon as he was half a mile downstream from the clearing, he looked for a place to rest. He had been lucky. By rights he ought to be dead. He held out his hand, watched it shake. This fight had not been any more strenuous than others he'd been involved in, yet he felt a deep exhaustion and a kind of inner anxiety he'd never had.

He followed a small tributary of the river into a glen. Under a thick stand of timber he found a niche where a log had fallen. He dropped the reins onto the ground to hold the grey then crawled into the leaf-lined hole. Slumping against the log he closed his bloodshot eyes.

His shoulder burned and his shirt was matted with dried blood. Good, that meant the wound was not deep. His arm bothered him more. Where he had rubbed it again and again against the rope it was scraped raw. He scooped up a pile of wet leaves and laying his arm on them, plastered the oozing welts.

He tried to rest but his mind kept re-running the feeling in his stomach. All these years he had been driven to find Simon. He had been tuned like a finely-strung instrument to make that one clear, demanding note: get Simon! And now he was close. So close he could taste the hot anger building up inside. Anger that had caused him to act rashly once already. He must not lose control again.

He shivered as he recalled that first encounter with Fetty. Pa, ashen-faced, stuffing the ring into his hand, Simon screaming for his help . . . instead swept up and carried off on that horse, that cursed Appaloosa stallion that pranced and pawed the air just as Fetty raised the shotgun!

Randlett shook his head. No good to dredge up memories. He had enough trouble tracking, didn't need to recall all those images.

He slept. When he opened his eyes it was morning. The rain clouds had cleared leaving a brilliant sky and a morning chorus of bluejays.

Damp and aching, bruised in a hundred places, Randlett crawled out of the hollow and carefully stretched his muscles. "Can't waste time sleeping the day away," he told the gelding who was munching pickle weed nearby.

Out of his pack Randlett took a rag and poured water on it from his canteen. He washed the bloody shoulder and flexed his muscle to loosen the edges of the swollen groove.

Then he dragged dead limbs for a small fire over which he boiled a hunk of venison with some wild onion roots he found near the edge of the stream. He ate the meat then drank the broth.

Climbing into the saddle was a chore. How he wanted to sit and rest . . . or sleep. But he dared not quit, not when he was so close. Bugs Harper and Soda McPherson were either after him or they were headed on into the lair.

He found out which within the hour.

His own tracks were near the incline to the hill where the fight had taken place. No other tracks overlapped his. Good, Randlett thought. They're going into hiding.

Cautious yet sure the outlaws were gone, he rode up to the body of O'Riley. The grey side-stepped and Randlett decided to leave the corpse, let Fetty come across his dead partner, see for himself the evil his stunt had caused.

He toed the grey across the top of the ridge, down the swale, and up again into the mountain canyon along the Yellow Cat. Their tracks were easy to follow in the damp sand. Even into the brush and trees he had no trouble following the two men.

He rode fast until he entered the dry-bottomed canyon itself. Then he settled into a walk, his eyes glancing right and left, high and low, as the walls of the canyon rose and opened into jagged fissures on each side.

The sun overhead brought with it a dull headache. His arm burned and his shoulder felt hot. Fever setting in after all.

Randlett studied the open country as he came out onto a ledge near the top of one of the side branches. Lon had said the Tepee was directly north of the middle hump in the low mountain range of the Fox Tails. That middle hump was now in sight. Of course Tepee Mesa itself was hidden from view. It could only be seen when you came through the narrow cut between that middle hump and its nearest neighboring peak. A waterfall tumbled from the higher ridge covering the opening. The opening was called Dripping Springs and it was passable if you didn't mind a little water.

Randlett shrugged. There was only one hitch. The Blood—that isolated, renegade branch captained by Red Vest, or whatever his name was—were camped in the valley south of Dripping Springs. They blocked anyone wanting to reach the Tepee. Stalking Deer, Randlett muttered to himself, why the devil couldn't you have helped.

Never mind. Maybe he'd get the robbers before they got to the Springs. Fetty and company should be camped somewhere on one of these ridges.

Topping the next salmon colored plateau, Randlett felt a prickling along the back of his neck. No one was in sight and he heard nothing except the snorting of the grey and crunch of gravel underfoot. But he was being followed.

He rounded a boulder and sat listening. He heard nothing. He studied the rocky terrain before him. Another series of narrow fissures split the higher canyon walls on his right.

Suddenly he sat straighter. Horse droppings seared in the heat not two feet from one of those fissures. He turned the gelding and followed the narrow gorge for two hundred yards . . . to a dead-end cul-de-sac.

Randlett turned in the saddle. He saw no movement or shadow but his heart beat a thundering tattoo. His instinct was never wrong about being trailed. Show yourself, he mumbled.

He had never felt so spooked. The grey gave no sign and he was usually first to know they were being followed. The memory of that lone rider splitting off to go to the McMillan ranch flitted through Randlett's mind and he shook his head to clear his thoughts.

Sweating profusely, Randlett eased off the canteen and

swallowed hot water. He moved to the shade of the wall and let the grey rest. He was certain the riders had entered this gorge. Where could they have gone. . . . ? Ah, he thought as he glanced at the ground ten feet away. The hoof-cut of a horse.

Randlett kneed the gelding to the other side of the outcrop. As he suspected, it turned into one of the side aisles that was not visible until you stood directly in front of it. The cut led up a steep grade directly toward the top of the canyon. Slowly Randlett reined into the cut, his eye now overhead.

The red clay walls on either side scraped his boots. The gelding halted, backtracked, and Randlett clucked softly to urge him on. Loose shale along the incline was no foothold for a thousand pound horse and the grey grumbled in his throat.

"Ho! boy," Randlett urged, and laid a boot heel into the grey's flanks before the horse would tackle any more of the shelf-like ledges. Snorting, bounding from one layer to another, his eyes white-rimmed, the gelding worked to stay clear of the walls which thankfully were widening as they neared the top.

More than half-way up, with shadowing pillars of hard grey slate on either side, Randlett suddenly stopped the gelding with an iron-fisted jerk. His blue eyes tightened to a thin slit. A vein throbbed in his temple.

Holding the grey to a precarious standstill, Randlett studied the opening ten feet above him. It was either up and out, or. . . . There was no way to back down. No room for the horse to turn. This is crazy, he thought. I'm trapped. The tracks of the outlaws had led him into a perfect one-man noose!

Deciding instantly, Randlett gouged his toes into the

horse's ribs and leaned forward in the saddle. The gelding lunged ahead, hooves scrambling for a foothold.

Five feet before the outlet, the grey whinnied to a terrified halt and Randlett's heart stood still.

He had been right, the gully was a trap and Leek Fetty himself was the captor. With the monogrammed double-barrel shotgun cradled insolently in his arms, the outlaw sat astride the silent Appaloosa stallion, blocking the passageway.

Randlett stared at the nightmare. A pain lanced down his left arm . . . the arm that wasn't there. But the palm of his right hand tingled with excitement and its fingers clenched the butt of the Colt.

Fetty grinned and the high sun sparked off the gun.

"Soda said you wus gonna be a hard maverick to turn back," the outlaw growled sullenly. "Decided to come see for myself. Might be better all round to go ahead and stomp you under once fer all. Hell, boy, you shoulda been dead the first time."

"I lived because I had to, Fetty," Randlett flared. "I had to stop that greedy appetite of yours. You have never been satisfied and never will as long as you live." He flicked his eyes to either side of the opening and caught the glint of a rifle on a high ridge to the right. Harper or McPherson. Maybe both.

Fetty's cool voice swaggered, "Too bad you couldn't've come up with the family coffers your old pa stashed away somewheres. Easy to tell by your look you haven't. Might been able to do some bargaining if you hada." Fetty touched the palouse and the grey's nervous response was to back further along the ledge, against the wall.

Randlett glared up at Fetty, asking, "That why you

kept Simon all these years under your murderin' thumb?"

The outlaw flinched but said slowly and deliberately, "The boy could go anytime."

An idea hit Randlett and he said, "Maybe you hoped he would and lead you to the Randlett money. Everyone has his uses, huh Fetty?"

The outlaw gigged the Appaloosa who danced near the edge of the fissure, knocking gravel downslope. Randlett smelled the hot, musty grain-breath of the stallion and the grey whickered a protest, slinging his big head, trying not to be forced back again.

Randlett snarled through gritted teeth, "The kid doesn't know anything about that treasure. I'm the one who knows!" He played his hand dangerously close but nothing he could say would matter now. His tone mocking, uncaring, Randlett added, "And I'm not about to tell."

The tight sun-burned skin on Fetty's face turned sallow as blood drained from it. No one denied Leek Fetty his wants. No one taunted the power to give or not give. That was Fetty's alone. Remembering the wasted years, his gut burning into morbid anger, Leek Fetty raised the shotgun and fired.

Chapter Fifteen

But he waited a split second too long. Randlett saw the change in Fetty and read what was coming. He swerved forward, over the side of the gelding. The blast knocked shale and sand into a powdery storm but only a few pellets nicked Randlett's ear and the gelding's rump.

Randlett raised up, staring at Fetty. Hot blood flooded his whole being. His eyes hardened into glassy blue nuggets of hate. Fetty on that horse! Fetty on that plunging, towering black and white monster. Fetty firing that shotgun!

Something in Randlett's gut snapped like the loosening of a coiled spring. Such anger and hate coursed through him he trembled. And it was clear to him now this was anger he'd harbored all these years was not simply for what Fetty had done to Simon. Now it was plain to Randlett the anger was also for himself. He wanted to get Fetty not just for stealing his brother, or for killing his father and mother. He wanted the man for what he had done to himself. He hated Fetty for taking his arm; for depriving him of the ability to live like other men, to do what other men could do, to accomplish the things he cherished and would never realize.

His hand caught at the colt . . . then as quickly held back. Smiling grimly, Randlett took a deep breath, leaned forward, and kicked the grey toward the top of the gully. Before the two horses collided, he had launched himself out of the saddle.

Using the gelding as a springboard, he dived into the Appaloosa's neck. Reaching up, clamping his fist onto the shotgun, Randlett twisted and pulled, jerking Fetty off the squealing horse.

The two men tumbled downslope, grappling together in a fury of hate, scraping and scalding bare arms and faces on the sharp stone of the fissure.

Somewhere a shot rang out. Rock near Randlett's head shattered and spewed gravel. Harper's carbine!

Randlett locked his legs around the sweat-damp body of Fetty who was struggling to level the shotgun. Another rifle shot tore a hole in Fetty's shirt and the man cursed and flung his head to one side trying to keep from getting hit.

Seeing his chance, Randlett followed the head-fling with a balled up fist aside Fetty's jaw. Fetty slumped into the wall and the shotgun slithered down the alley.

Randlett's leg's unlocked from around Fetty's limp body and he lurched up onto his knees. Now two rifle shots—McPherson and Harper both—peppered the wall over Randlett and he knew the next one would find him.

Then from the heart of the canyon, echoing from wall to wall, a long blood-curdling cry broke the hot air.

Randlett felt a jolt of surprise . . . and fierce pride . . . as he listened to the exultant war cry of Tom Stalking Deer.

The countering rifles on the heights above churned the air with defiant exchanges as Fetty and Randlett struggled to keep from falling further down the gully, struggling to stay clear of the hooves of the grey. The big gelding was wild-eyed in a frenzy of fear, unable to gain a foothold.

Randlett finally braced himself on a protruding rock and grabbing the outlaw, stood with feet astride Fetty as he blinked up in bewilderment. The man glanced around for the shotgun, realized it was gone and began to grovel backward toward a level place along the edge.

Randlett let him reach the safety of the ledge before he laid another fist into the man's chest. Fetty gasped and turned away. Randlett yanked him up, let him fall back, and before he could hit the ground laid that same fist aside his neck.

"Git up and fight," Randlett snarled. Sweat dripped into the blood on his chin and he struck a boot to Fetty's backside as the outlaw squirmed upright.

Randlett glanced down, watching with a knot in his throat as the grey back-slid further and further down the slope. "He'll break a leg," Randlett grumbled. Then with anger blazing from his eyes he turned back toward the outlaw.

Fetty held to the crumbling red wall, sputtering, spitting, drooling from his open mouth.

"Never fought man to man?" Randlett demanded and cocked a grinning eye toward the shots coming from overhead. They began to sound farther and farther away. So much for faithful cohorts!

"Wait . . ." garbled Fetty, putting one hand in front of his face.

"No more waiting, Fetty. This is it!" And the one-armed man swung a slashing uppercut into that face.

Blood spurted. Fetty howled and slumped against the wall. He flailed and groaned and got another kick in the ribs.

Fetty rolled into a ball. Then cursing, he opened one eye, glanced up, and shivered at what he saw. The one-armed man standing over him was his death. Fetty was thunderstruck. He couldn't believe he'd lost his cherished gun. He couldn't believe a one-armed man had yanked him away from his stallion. He began to cry.

"You'll not get away with that!" Randlett muttered and again pulled him upright as he laid a knee into the outlaw's flabby stomach.

Fetty fell onto Randlett's legs and closing his eyes pulled with a last dogged effort.

Caught by surprise, Randlett toppled backward and began sliding downslope under the gelding's thrashing hooves. The grey whinnied, his rear hooves splayed outward and he began to slide faster down the layered shale. Randlett watched in horror as the horse, now belly-down, floundered all the way to the bottom of the cul-de-sac, his whistling scream rending the air.

Randlett shot his gaze upward. He had stopped himself with a boot wedged against a crack. He was now a good eight feet below Fetty.

Fetty was now standing, staring down, his mouth a mass of pulp, his cheeks and eyes in a strut.

But what caught Randlett's eye was the shotgun. It lay between the two men, stuck in a crevice, five feet from Randlett, two feet from Fetty.

Together they stared at the weapon. It sparkled in the sun, its carved silver F showing the intricate details of its beauty.

Randlett was mesmerized. Squinting against the blinding sun, he riveted his sight on Fetty. Then as a sour grin broke the tension of Randlett's bruised lips he realized their predicament. The shotgun was still between them . . . that great equalizer still existed to haunt Randlett's revenge. Fair enough, he reflected. Fair enough.

A blur of movement was all Fetty saw as Randlett plowed upward, fingers curling in anticipation. But he did not grab the gun. Instead he flicked out a boot, sending it scooting impotently down the alley, a hundred feet below . . .

Terror froze Fetty. He knew his fate. And Randlett was merciless. He was up on his feet in a heart's breath, lunging at Fetty, dropping the outlaw like a sack of rotten potatoes. Without let-up he began to pound his face and body with blows from his doubled-up fist.

Randlett kicked and beat, recalling with each blow the hurt and death he and his family and others had suffered at the hands of this monster.

Suddenly a bullet clipped a wedge off the rock overhead. Another slug kicked dust off the wall. Randlett jerked to attention. . . .

A rider at the top, riding a small pinto mustang and raising a rifle over his head, urged the pony down the shale-layered alley.

"Go!" Tom Stalking Deer commanded as he slid off the pinto and struggled to pull Randlett away from the outlaw's bloody body. "They will return. . . ."

Randlett swayed, daubed a wet ear and spat. Then in a daze he followed the Indian to the bottom of the alley where they found the grey standing, trembling but unhurt.

Randlett swung up. Stalking Deer wheeled around and led the way, splashing through the watery ribbon of the Yellow Cat all the way out of the canyon . . . all the way to the Bitter Weed Divide.

Chapter Sixteen

Randlett was now in the lead. He was heading for the lodge of Sun Woman. The Indian protested but Randlett paid no attention. "That side of yours needs herbs which grow only in the marsh and I cannot tend the fever that is at this very moment replacing your wits," Randlett advised.

Stalking Deer made a furtive motion to lessen the pain of his side by pinching the muscle of his upper thigh. Randlett frowned. He had not noticed the wound until Stalking Deer had nearly fallen from his horse. They were at the edge of the Buffalo Hollow Hills. Once across the field of yellow bitter weeds they would be safe.

If Harper or McPherson had known the Indian was wounded they surely would have given chase. But perhaps Fetty demanded care first. That is, if he was alive. Randlett had no idea if he had really hurt the man . . . whether Fetty was dead or merely out of commission for a dew days. He only knew he felt free. In fact he would be happy never to touch his pistol or use his fists again. The release of that anger had been a balm.

Maybe Fetty would quit, let Simon go, he reasoned. Or at least be so weak in leadership that Simon could break away.

The late sun was a faint glow at their backs when they rode into the cool shadows of a cypress grove. Stalking Deer's eyes were already bright with fever but his mind turned to Randlett. "Did you kill the white dog?" he asked.

"I don't know, Stalking Deer. For me he is dead unless he continues to hold Simon."

"Tom!" growled the irate Indian. "I am Tom Stalking Deer."

Randlett closed his eyes and sighed. He felt great affection for his friend and now realized how much this name-identity with the white man's world meant to him. "Tom!" Randlett said with gusto. "Son of Stands Around, Chief of the peace-seeking Cheyenne of the Great Fox Tails. You are Tom Stalking Deer."

A flicker of a smile crossed the Indian's lips. No brave smiles at his own coup but Tom Stalking Deer came close. His pony quickened his pace and he swayed over the stubby neck, caught himself and grunted a Cheyenne curse at the blundering horse. "If the white man lives he will not be the same, Man Alone. He will be as the wolf who carries within his carcass an arrow. . . ."

Randlett's feeling of elation disappeared. Stalking Deer was right. His responsibility to stop Fetty was not going to be solved with a simple fist fight.

Three men carried Stalking Deer into the Chief's lodge. He was laid on a pile of buffalo robes with a spirit-smoke of dried mullein burning near his head.

Sun Woman cleaned the wound and Magpie sought

willow twigs to make a fever-tea and marsh herbs to prevent infection. Her dark eyes were full of questions but she bent over the sleeping Indian and began to pack the ugly wound with pulverized leaves.

"I told you he would come back," Randlett said, holding Stalking Deer's shoulder as he thrashed in pain. "If he hadn't followed me and joined the fight I would be buzzard bait right now."

Magpie's lovely face relaxed at his "American" expression. "Then Stalking Deer is a man of honor," she said and her smile faded.

"Yes. Tom Stalking Deer is a man of honor."

Randlett stayed two days. By the second morning Stalking Deer was sitting up, talking, eating steaks cut from the haunches of the scarce buffalo. Stands Around sat with crossed arms before his fire, listening with pride as his wayward son told how he had tracked this white brother in secret and been ready to join the fight.

Randlett was heartened by his red brother's reception. A gathering of young braves and old men listened to his tale with nods and wide eyes. Maybe after a time Magpie's affection would change, he told himself. After all, Stalking Deer belonged here. He should be the one to take this lovely young woman as his mate not the half brother . . . the half-white, half-Indian man who really knew neither world as a man should. Randlett smiled at that thought. Yes, life in the white world was beyond him now too. Why, he hadn't read a book in ten years, he knew nothing of politics or government, doubted if he could carry on a decent conversation with a town man.

Magpie wore the necklace he had brought before and she went several times a day to the pool to admire the gold beads on her smooth brown throat. Randlett found her there and talked. Later, they sat beside Stalking Deer in the lodge. He was solemn and watchful but with Magpie's attention on him again he was not openly jealous.

Randlett found himself weighing Magpie in his mind's eye as a woman . . . against other women. Or maybe against another woman. He knew Magpie still loved him but he now had hope that she would come to accept Stalking Deer.

Late the third day Randlett decided to leave. Sheriff Draper might know about the fight by now. And there was the dance. Randlett was excited about meeting Suede . . . Simon. He was determined to meet that young man and clear up the mystery of who he was.

It was Thursday noon when he rode into Wolfe City. He needed to be in town to make contact with Suede Carson if possible before the dance. So he booked a room in the hotel.

He left the gelding at the livery and the hostler assured him the shindig was on for tonight.

Randlett sauntered down the boardwalk. He noticed men stringing lanterns around a one-hundred-foot square platform at the far end of town. Families in buggies were already arriving. Single men swarmed in on horseback and people gathered in gossiping clots all over town. He saw no one who might possibly be his brother.

Sheriff Draper was not in his office and after asking a few men, Randlett found out the sheriff had plans to 'let the law circulate' until after the dance. Meaning he would not be in his office until tomorrow.

Randlett went to his room in the town's two-story hotel. He was led to a ten-by-twelve stuffy hole with a sagging bed and a low dresser with a cracked mirror.

He sat down on the bed, deciding he might take a cap-nap but it had been ten years since he had been in a room and thinking about sleeping in a bed gave him an urge to bolt.

But, he reasoned, he could give it a try. He lay back, cradled his head on his arm with his feet sticking over the end of the cot. He grinned. He knew it all the time. He didn't fit. Not in this white man's tight, ready-made world.

Going over to the fly-speckled mirror he studied his reflection. Hair too long. Clothes made from the wilds with a hat and boots of raw leather. At the dance he would look like the hayseed he was. And what would Abby McMillan's reaction be?

Well, he'd always wanted to see what he would look like in store-boughts. Maybe now was the time.

At the Mercantile, Randlett was fitted with a pair of chocolate brown twill pants, a matching tan vest with the same brown piping, a snowy white shirt and a slim string tie. Then the clerk found a pair of his best calfskin boots, medium heels. So shiny they didn't need spit.

"Amazing," the clerk commented. "You'll have every lady at the dance fallin' over in a swoon."

Randlett paid with a handful of gold nuggets which the man weighed out on a small drawer-scale. Then he went several doors down for a shave and bath. The barber trimmed his long hair into the latest style and gave him a cake of soap 'on special'.

Randlett soaked in a tub of tepid water, rubbed dry and put on the new clothes. The pants were stiff and scratched his legs but the shirt was comfortable if strange. He'd never get used to the hard-soled boots. Outside, at the startling clomp of their heels on the boardwalk, Randlett halted. He looked around. No one stared. Self-consciously he entered Bain's candy store and came away chewing on a piece of licorice. First he'd ever eaten.

By the time he got back to his hotel he'd had several men tip their hats in friendly camaraderie. And not one but at least three young ladies stared his way with bold admiration.

When he returned to the tiny room it was late and sultry hot. In front of the cracked mirror he looked like a stranger. He felt more of a misfit than ever. Maybe later he would wear the new getup, right now he needed to feel comfortable. He got back into his heelless soft skin boots and his deerskin pants. The white shirt and string tie looked good enough with his old pants so he left them on. Sighing, he stretched out on the cot and closed his eyes.

He woke to the sound of fiddling. The tune bounced into his darkening room from the open window. He lay for a moment listening, imagining how it must feel to be free of death and dying and revenge—how it must feel to be going to a party with nothing to worry about except twirling a lady to the music and eating Aunt Hannah's fried chicken.

Maybe tonight would be the end of his search. Surely when he saw Si . . . Suede Carson . . . face to face, he could work out any problem, even if it meant going directly to Sheriff Draper and keeping the boy in safe custody until they could go out with a posse and collect the rest of the gang. How old would he be now? Nineteen? Randlett's heart pounded with anticipation.

Swinging off the cot, he grabbed his sweat stained hat. Nodding sadly at the shiny boots in the corner he bounded out the door.

The galling heat of the day had gone with the sun. The town was refreshed. It had come alive with folk:

kids, young people, old timers, each louder and happier than the next, poured through the streets and headed for the platform at the south end of town.

Randlett watched as food was ladled out onto make-do tables under the trees. The board planks groaned with pies, cakes, buckets of stew and beans, jars of pickles and tomatoes, slabs of beef and venison, and chickens roasted and decorated with hardcooked eggs. Barrels of cider and lemonade sat underneath the tables and someone had rigged an iron lever over a firepit that held a five gallon pot of coffee.

He spotted Abby McMillan setting a basket of food down on one of the tables. As he approached he called her name and she whirled ecstatically, about to embrace him, her face so close to his he could feel her warm breath. She checked herself when she recognized him and a funny look flashed across her face.

"Think I was Suede?" he asked, gazing directly into her faltering eyes. "Brothers usually have the same voice quality you know."

She didn't answer but began to unpack her food. Her dress was of a swishy, rose-colored material that made her bare shoulders glow in the lamplight. "You won't forget will you . . . about introducing him," he said.

"No." She sounded angry.

"Have you seen him since we talked?"

"Once . . . very quickly. But he assured me he is coming and I told him about you . . . again . . . that I'd talked to you and that you wanted to meet him tonight. So it's all set and I hope it gets settled. But I'll not go hunting you up so you'd better stay around."

"Plan to." Couples were gathering on the platform and waltzing to the music. "I suppose Suede's a dandy on the dance floor. Simon would be," Randlett commented as they were forced away from the table by a surge of new-comers. They stood watching the dancers.

"Yes, we've danced several times at the house. While he sang and hummed," she said proudly.

"I'd ask you to dance myself, but I reckon sashaying around with a one-armed 'ombre might be a little embarrassing."

For once she looked frankly at him without the usual defensive barrier. "I don't think so, Mr. Randlett."

A tall, tow-headed young cowpoke interrupted and asked for the pleasure and she was swept away, her eyes still on Randlett.

He watched as she was traded from one partner to another until she had danced at least twice with every man on the floor. Breathless, she finally broke away and came out for a cup of cider. Randlett brought her a plate of food and they sat together under one of the trees.

"What time did he say he was coming?" he asked. A pressure was building in his chest the more he thought about this meeting with his brother.

"He . . . he should be here any minute. Suede's not concerned with time, you see. He's very independent." She was defensive again.

"Guess I can wait," Randlett answered, but he noticed she kept looking to the far corners of the crowd as she went back to the dance. He was beginning to doubt this Suede Carson would show.

He had just accepted a piece of pie from an elderly lady who couldn't bear to see anyone 'stand around not eating', when a kid came up. Staring at his empty sleeve he asked, "You Randlett?"

"Yes."

"The man says he'll see you at the livery." Having

delivered his message the boy skipped over to the cakes and grabbed the biggest slice he could find.

Randlett checked on Abby. She was involved with a group of dancers in a long line, holding up her skirt with one hand, the other locked onto the one next to her. He should have time to see about 'that man' and be back before they ended the kick.

His palm was damp as he strode toward the livery. The lane was deserted and the stable was dark except for a single lantern at the open door.

No man waited at the entrance. No one was in front, no one in the hall. Randlett sauntered in, glancing into the stalls on either side. The grey neighed and he went up to scratch his nose. The boy must have gotten a wrong message. Or maybe it was a dodge to get him away from the dance.

He turned, was about to move toward the door when a shadow rose up from behind. A sharp blow over the left ear dropped Randlett like a lead bullet. He pitched over into the straw without uttering a sound.

Chapter Seventeen

The young cowboy dancing with Abby McMillan was spellbound. She talked about food, about the music, about this year's dance as compared to last year's, but her attention was elsewhere.

Where is Suede, she wondered, her eyes raking the crowd. He promised. He simply had to come. She would never be able to face that man Kane Randlett if he didn't.

And where was Randlett? He had been by the cider table and now he was gone. She flashed a glance and saw an old man standing in Randlett's place.

When the music stopped she nodded to the young man who was her partner. Dabbing a handkerchief over her cheeks, she strode off the platform.

Her father was talking to Bill Jernigan and . . . and she couldn't believe it. Suede Carson, immaculately groomed, as cool as if he'd never seen a horse, stood talking to the small group of men. He held them, telling one of his 'poker game' stories.

"Abby gal," Pat McMillan beamed, turning to his daughter. "Suede's lookin' for you."

"I've been right here for the last three hours," she clipped.

Carson's smile never wavered. Winking at the men, he steered her away. "Sorry I couldn't get here sooner, honey. I got tied up in a business deal. There'll be lots of time yet for dancing and I can't wait to give you a whirl. But first let's talk."

He motioned toward a bench on the walk in front of a store. June beetles dived in and out of the glow cast by an overhead lamp. Abby breathed deeply, savoring the warm night air. Too bad Kane Randlett had disappeared just when Suede arrived but she had no more obligation to him. Now she could relax and enjoy the evening.

"Suede, what sort of business deal was it. You've never talked about what you do. . . ."

Suede Carson's hungry look traveled over her face and shoulders. Grinning, he pulled her to him and kissed her mouth, then her bare shoulder. She stiffened.

"Okay, beautiful, you win." He let her go but kept his eyes on her lips. "As a matter of fact the deal has to do with you . . . with us. I've just bought a house and invested in a nice little business in St. Louis. In a week or two we'll be ready to leave."

"Wh . . . what do you mean?' Abby McMillan's forehead wrinkled in a deep frown.

"That's where we're going to live after we're married. You know I've always wanted to get out of here. Well, the time is . . . things are working out so that we can leave sooner than I thought.

"You'll love St. Louis. It's a *real* town and the house is very nice."

"Suede! I . . . you haven't even asked me, and I'm not sure I want to live anywhere but here."

"Don't be silly. Wolfe City has nothing to offer after you've seen St. Louis. But we can be married here. I know how much you've always wanted to be married at the Double M. And I want our marriage to start off right."

He smiled and Abby could not resist its mischief and devotion. "A few weeks?" she asked, her mind already whirling in a dozen directions.

"Sure, why not. And just to make it official, to keep you thinking about it, here's something I want you to wear."

Abby looked up. His voice was different. It had a mellow quality, nearly sad. She had never seen him so still, so serious. He took her hand and gently unfolded it. He slipped a ring on one finger. She had not seen where it came from.

"It's not a regular promise ring, Abby, but it's special to me and I'd like you to wear it."

She could barely see the ring in the shadows and through her misty eyes, but she didn't care what it looked like. Suede could be tender, could be sentimental and loving after all. He really wanted her to marry him.

A strange release of happiness filled her breast and she reached up and kissed him. She rose then and twirled around, her hand held out before her. "I love it," she crooned. "Let's dance, Suede. I feel like I could waltz all night!"

They walked into the shadows toward the music. Randlett was still nowhere to be seen but the little old man was still there. She and Suede waltzed all the way around the floor and back. She looked again. The old man was still there and he was watching . . . intently watching every movement Suede Carson made.

Randlett crawled awake. He touched his head and whistled as pain shot through his neck and jaw. He sat up, rubbing his neck, trying not to touch the egg raised near that left ear.

Squinting in the semi-darkness of the livery lanterns, he stared in front of him. He was outside under two trees. They moved and became one, then divided into two again.

Unsteady as a new-born colt, Randlett staggered upright. He closed his eyes, waiting for the dizziness to end.

His head ached but his mind was clear. Someone wanted him out of the way, did not intend for him to meet Suede Carson.

Anger rising inside, Randlett headed for the end of main street. He hoped the party was still going on.

Near the dance platform he sagged against a roof-post. Damn! The dance was over, only a few scragglers were left packing up.

Abby, where was Abby McMillan? He scanned the meager crowd and couldn't find her.

Then she was in front of him. Ignoring his disheveled appearance, she grabbed his hand and pulled him nearer the lantern light. She thrust her own white and slightly shaking hand into the light and announced, "He came, Mr. Randlett. I'm sorry you weren't here, but he came and we danced, and it was perfect. He gave me this."

He fought to stay afoot and a shiver went through his whole body when he saw the ring. It was enormous. It was no engagement ring. It had a green and black and ivory configuration in a gold setting so huge it covered her whole finger.

He felt weak. He knew that ring. He knew without looking closer that it was the family crest of Jonathon Niles Randlett. It was the ring Leek Fetty had coveted, that he wanted so desperately he shot off the arm of the eldest son.

"You . . . you two are promised?" Randlett finally managed.

"Yes. In just a few weeks we'll be married. He has a new business in St. Louis and we'll live there."

Randlett swayed against the pole. "You want to do that?"

"Yes . . . I want to marry Suede."

"No, I mean move to St. Louis."

"I . . . a wife has to go where her husband can find work, Mr. Randlett."

He realized he would not be able to talk to Abby McMillan about the ring . . . not tonight. She was too thrilled thinking she would be the wife of Suede Carson.

His head felt like one of those split melons under the table. He couldn't think straight. "Abby, I need to talk to you. I'll ride out to the Double M tomorrow . . . okay?"

"Surely, Mr. Randlett," she fairly bubbled. Then she gathered her basket and headed for the Double M wagon.

Dragging leaden feet, Randlett made it to his hotel room where he fell asleep as soon as he untied the leggings on his boots.

Chapter Eighteen

Randlett took a deep breath of the bright, sunny morning air. The road to the Double M meandered through beautiful country and it always helped him settle his worries to be in the saddle on such a day.

A patch of berries along the side drew buzzing honey bees and the perfume of wild honeysuckle along the creekbed mingled with the dusty odor of sand. It reminded him of when he was a kid back east with his family. He wondered if Simon could remember those days. And by the by, why didn't the boy want to meet him last night?

The vision of that ring flashed into Randlett's mind and he sighed. Simon had the ring! Simon—it had to be Simon—had the Randlett family ring! That knowledge had knocked him for a loop. How did the kid get the ring? He wondered. Fetty would know he had it so he couldn't have pinched it from Fetty's catch. That meant only one thing, Fetty had given it to Simon. But why? Randlett did not want to think about that.

Abby McMillan was wearing a faded blue cotton dress, the sleeves rolled up above her elbows. Flour dusted her hands and nose. Her face was flushed from the heat of the stove and her hair was awry. Randlett's stomach did a flip-flop when she touched his arm, urging him into the kitchen with a brilliant smile.

She had cooked her best meal: smothered chicken, field peas, and apple pie. Hot biscuits would be ready in minutes. Randlett had not thought of eating but as the food was put on the table and the three work hands came in, slickered over and eager-eyed, he joined with pleasure.

Abby and her father presided over the meal like a father and mother over a brood of skinny children, offering another helping or another biscuit or more dessert until the children shook heads and pushed back from the table with groans.

When the hands excused themselves Abby and her father fell to talk. After a few moments Randlett forgot his shyness and found himself speaking about farm life and neighbors . . . and then they were asking about his own family.

"My father was a teacher," he said, "in a university. But he was never satisfied with living in the East, teaching people who already had learning opportunities. Pa wanted to offer the man 'out there' as he used to say, a knowledge about history and other civilizations. It was as strong as a religious calling for him."

Abby sipped her tea, watching him closely as he spoke of his family. He wondered if she was thinking this might be Suede's family too.

Pat McMillan bit off the end of a cigar and leaned back in his chair. "That why you headed West?"

"Yes, sir. My mother knew Pa would never be content

until he tried it. So we foolishly trekked out into some pretty wild country, completely innocent and unprepared." Randlett looked at Abby and added, "Simon was ripping to come west. He was a kid who loved adventure. He was unhappy at home, he craved new things and he enjoyed being the center of attention. Had a fearsome temper too that could flash out of his perky face like a raging storm.

"Maybe he still has it." Randlett never took his eyes from Abby's face. When she turned away without comment he looked at Pat McMillan and said, "I guess Abby's told you, sir, that I believe Suede Carson is my brother."

The man nodded vigorously. "Yes. Yes, and even though she says she doesn't believe it, I can see it might be possible. It's been a very unusual courtship and I've not got a handle on the boy yet. Seems he can't stay still for much scrutiny."

Randlett now stared at the ring on Abby's left hand. "That ring he gave her last night is the one my father was slipping into my hand when we were ambushed."

Abby McMillan's face paled. Her eyes grew large and instinctively she closed her other hand over the ring.

The men waited for her to speak. Slowly unfolding her hand, she spread her fingers against the white tablecloth revealing the huge ivory and green encrusted ring.

Randlett leaned over and pointed. "You can see the initials of my father if you look closely. There's a J and an N on either side. The R is in the middle. Those colors are on several other family heirlooms. Were, that is. The rest of our things were lost with the money we were carrying."

Her father took the ring, turned it over, examined it. "Why would this Suede . . . or Simon if it is your brother . . . give Abby the ring and yet not care about getting in touch with you?"

"I can't figure that out, Mr. McMillan, except I'm certain he can't leave the gang. I believe Fetty holds some threat over him. He may even be using my life as a threat now that Simon knows I'm here.

"Or. . . ." and he said this with reservation but he had to say it, "he may be using Abby's life as a hold since Simon cares for her."

Pat McMillan stuck his cigar into a coffee cup where it sizzled angrily. Abby sent a hostile stare at both men then began nervously stacking plates as she said, "Suede is no outlaw! He's sweet and kind and whatever he does for a living I'm sure it's honorable."

"Now, Ab," said her father, "we're not accusing him of anything. It's just that we can't seem to get him rope-tied. He's a slippery critter of sorts and I'd like my son-in-law to be a might more stable."

The men rose. Giving compliments to the cook they went out to the porch. McMillan led the way to the far side, out of hearing of his daughter. He looked worried.

"Randlett, I'll put it to you straight. I don't like this a little bit. She's falling faster and deeper ever day for that kid. Come in last night saying he wants to marry her in a few weeks then cart her off to the big city. Guess you know how that makes me feel. I always counted on Abby stayin' here."

McMillan stuck a new cigar into his mouth and added, "I'm durned if I can do anything, Randlett. Can't really get close to that boy to confront him and I have no way of tracing him from any other angle. What can I do?"

"That's why I rode out here today, Mr. McMillan. I'd like to try something. And I need your help."

"I'll do anything if it'll answer some questions. Two of my men are fair guns and I'm not a slouch myself."

"That would only get a lot of us killed. What I'm thinking is maybe a safer bet, though it's all risky. You'll have to risk some money. A lot."

"Name it. I have some."

Randlett admired the rancher's quick, plain-spoken reply. He hoped his plan would merit such trust. "I understand you've sometimes had money staged from the Conger City Bank to pay for large cattle buys. That right?"

"Yes, it is."

"Then send for a large sum to be transferred here. And make sure Simon . . . Suede Carson . . . knows about it. I'm certain Simon is being used as the go-between. The way I figure, he supplies the information about what and when to hit. Can you let him know without Abby finding out?"

"Probably. I'll have to be lucky and be here when he happens by."

"Then just wait until he shows. Mention your shipment and set the date right then."

"You think he'll bite?" McMillan asked.

"If it's tasty enough Fetty will bite," Randlett said with a dry laugh.

"We'll make it tasty enough, Randlett."

"Just don't let Abby know we're deliberately telling Simon about the shipment."

"Count on it."

Chapter Nineteen

Suede Carson watched Abby's father leave the Double M ranch. Slipping from his perch on a rise south of the house, Carson stepped into the saddle of a beautiful pale gold horse. He cantered easily, circled to the front and tied the horse to the rail. He whistled melodically as he slid off.

Abby McMillan was at the door as soon as he put a shiny black boot on the step. As he grabbed her in an embrace and began to cover her face with kisses she stiffened. Oblivious to her mood, he nodded toward the stallion and asked, "Like him?"

She walked to the end of the porch taking in the magnificence of the graceful animal. "Suede, how in the world can you afford such a. . . ."

"Told you I'd get fixed up some day soon and that day is here." He pulled off a pair of tight suede gloves, a piece of finery he always wore. He had on a pair of beige pants tucked into the black boots with designs in grey leather along the sides. His shirt was blue silk. The horse was saddled with a black and grey saddle over a blanket of the same dark blue as his shirt.

"Oh, Suede, I can't keep up with you," Abby began but he interrupted. "Don't try, Abby, just set the date for two weeks from today for us to get married. I can't wait to get back East where we can do things and meet some decent people."

"Two weeks? So soon?" She was incredulous.

"Not getting cold feet are you?" he chided as they went inside. They crossed into the parlor. Abby made him sit on the stiff horsehair sofa while she went to get refreshments. She poured lemonade and offered him a piece of cake.

Coming to a conclusion she said, "Suede, listen. I have something to ask . . . to talk about."

He smiled wickedly. Then seeing her worry he complied with, "Okay, what?"

"This ring. That man Kane Randlett says this is . . . is an old family heirloom of his family. He says it bears the initials of his family. Look, it does have a J and an N and this in the middle is an R."

Suede Carson's mouth turned down in a what-if attitude. "Maybe it is. I won it in a card game. I forget where."

Seeing her dismay he dropped the fork and grabbed her hand. "Mi vida, you are always so worried, so full of questions."

When she closed her eyes he suddenly flushed in anger, "You don't seem to believe me. Or to trust me, Abby."

"Oh, Suede, it's not that. It's just this man keeps saying. . . ."

"What?" he growled with a tinge of red lighting his

blue eyes. "What does he say?" He began to pace the floor, his hands rubbing his arms as if he were cold.

She went to him, put her palm against his hot cheek. "Suede, are you in trouble?"

His short, lithe body relaxed. Bringing himself under control he placed his hands on her shoulders. "No," he answered gently, "I'm not in trouble. That's why I say set the date. I'll be able to come for you in two weeks. Okay?"

A footstep sounded in the front hall. Turning, they saw her father stride into the room.

"Well, hello, Mr. Carson," Pat McMillan said, his voice friendly and open. He cautiously watched the young man's reaction to his unexpected entrance. Carson merely nodded.

"Oh, Dad," Abby cried. She was thrilled. Now her father could have his talk with Suede. She smiled at Suede, her eyes telling him to make the first move.

"Sir," Carson began, "with your permission we've just decided to be married two weeks from today." He winked at Abby, his old overwhelming confidence ruling the day.

"Hmmm," McMillan murmured, going to the sideboard for a cigar. He lit the long black tobacco roll with a slow, steady hand then glanced at his daughter over the curling smoke. "You want that, Ab, girl?" he asked simply.

"I . . . yes," she said firmly, reacting to the plea and expectancy on Suede's face.

"You able to support a wife, Mr. Carson?" McMillan queried as any good father should.

"Yes, sir. I'll be a partner in a trade-goods business in St. Louis. Papers aren't signed yet so I can't speak of the details, but it's a good thing. We'll be wanting to move there. But we'll be wed in Wolfe City. And I'd prefer, sir, right here in your home."

Abby frowned a little but nodded silently.

Pat McMillan dusted ashes off his decaying cigar. "Then that will work out fine with what we've been talking about. Abby was wanting to go to Conger to visit her aunt for a few days so now I guess she'll have some special shopping to do, huh, girl?"

Abby stared. She could not believe how easily her father had been persuaded.

"Since her mother died my sister has been the one to help Abby with clothes and such," her father continued. Then turning to Abby he said, "Ab, go get that brandy in the kitchen. And those long thin glasses of your ma's. We'll celebrate."

As she left the room Pat McMillan said, "Yes, sir, my boy, she'll get the right help about the whys and whattos concernin' a wedding from Pearl. Women need to have things right, Carson. Particulars mean a lot to them. And they cost too, boy, they cost. But I expect that. Don't have a daughter to get married every day of the year and I want the best for Abby.

"Fact is," he waved the cigar in the air, "I was wanting Abby to go to Conger so's she can cash out some bonds for me. I'm plannin' to fence my east two hundred, you see, and I need the cold hard to hire ol' Franklin and his sons to do it."

He paused, clucking at the high cost of the deal. "Gonna take a chunk of my savings, but a fence will allow that field to become a fine meadow and I need winter grass."

Suede Carson nodded. "Investments like that pay off. You'll not be putting your money in a bad place. What day will Abby be going, sir?"

"Planned for her to leave day after tomorrow."

"She'll be coming back with the money? That's a little risky isn't it, sir?" Carson seemed worried.

"Oh no. I want her to get in a little vacation while she's there, as well as the shopping, so she'll be staying on. I'll have her send the money back on a special stage. Done that before you know.

"Say, are you interested in ranching, Carson?"

"A little, Mr. McMillan. But not enough to live on one. I'm afraid I'm a city man at heart."

"Born in a city?"

Before he could answer Abby came in with a tray and they drank a hearty toast to the coming marriage.

Pat McMillan thought his daughter looked a little peaked.

Tying his best bay gelding beside the buckskin and grey, McMillan joined the two men hunkered before a small fire.

"Have some coffee," Kane Randlett said. He stood up and handed the rancher a tin cup.

"Thanks. Is this the third man?" McMillan asked. He sipped the black syrup as he eyed the Indian across the fire.

"Yes. Tom Stalking Deer, Pat McMillan." The men looked at one another, taking time to make judgement. McMillan turned to gaze at the camp. "You boys are sleeping rough."

Randlett nodded. "We're used to it and it's handier this way. Besides," and he grinned, "I tried my hand sleeping in a real bed just the other day. They don't make 'em for a body tall enough to see over a breakin' pen."

McMillan raised an eyebrow, sizing up Randlett's six foot three frame. "Reckon you could be right." He threw grounds into the flame and said, "I'd like to join you on this trick, Randlett. You need more'n three men."

"If it works, three will be plenty from this end. It's Draper's responsibility to go and Tom here understands English except when he's told 'no'. And, I guess he deserves another crack at that bunch anyway." Randlett looked at the Indian who had convinced him he was fully recovered, well enough to hunt dogs.

Randlett addressed McMillan. "The two drivers know everything?"

"Yes. They know everything I told 'em . . . which was to keep down, not pull a rifle unless they have to in pure self defence. They know one of the raiders is to be given a chance to escape and that they are to take their signals from you when you show. They're a couple of touch guns, Randlett, I paid a friend in Conger to send 'em to Sheriff Marlin."

McMillan scowled. "You sure you can handle them bushwhackers, Randlett?"

Randlett waited a moment then said, "We'll be sitting . . . waiting . . . right before that damn curve on the Pass where they've hit twice already. We'll take them just as they ride in, before they've had a chance to draw fire."

The rancher was silent and Randlett continued. "It's enough to use your money. I don't want you in any more of a spot. If this fails, if the gang somehow gets away with the money, that will be a good price for you to pay."

"Don't think about the money, Randlett. I've got as much at stake as you. My girl is about to get tied up with that . . . sorry, Randlett."

Randlett shrugged, "I understand. But don't worry.

Just tell us all you can about Suede Carson. What does he look like?"

McMillan pushed his hat back off a damp forehead. "Well, he's half a head shorter'n you, Randlett . . . and by gum he has a look about him that reminds a body of you. 'Course I never noticed it before but now that you say he may be your brother, I can see he favors you. He's got short hair with sideburns and they're black same's his hair . . . same's yours."

Tom Stalking Deer listened with his hands on his thighs, his legs folded up under his torso. "His horse?" he asked.

"Well, the last time I saw him he was riding a fine, gaited palomino stallion. My boys say he also rides a red with black stockings."

Randlett began to douse the fire. "I'll go in and inform the Sheriff." He stopped to gaze at McMillan. "Abby knows nothing about this, right? And she will stay in Conger until you send word."

"You needn't worry about Abby. When she and Pearl get together with money and a reason for buying clothes . . . well, she'll be busy as long as this lasts."

"Good. I feel bad about doing this but as far as I can see it's the best way. To flush Fetty out in the open where we might be able to get Simon away. This may be the chance Simon has been waiting for."

Chapter Twenty

Randlett rode in by himself to see Sheriff Draper. The Indian and Draper were not to meet until the last minute since the Sheriff was convinced Stalking Deer should be brought in and punished for his wild ways. Randlett knew jail would kill the young buck. After this play was over there would be enough time to urge Stalking Deer to mend his ways.

Draper was nailing a wanted poster to the wall when Randlett stepped into his office. A few days ago when he had told Draper about the trap he planned he'd been surprised when the man said, "I want in on this." Randlett had presented the cold facts, thinking Draper would back down but the sheriff remained strong about wanting to be one of the three men waiting at the pass.

Now, as Randlett entered the office he was struck by the sheriff's expression. Will Draper was not the same arrogant toad he'd been before Lon's death. He had changed. A spot of grey ran through his shock of dark hair. His eyes glistened not with certainty but with a nervous twitter.

"I'm glad you decided to give me a . . . to let the law in on this, Randlett," Draper started. He blinked and Randlett wondered if he was about to cry. "No, I will be truthful. I do mean I'm glad you decided to give me another chance. I've realized lately what a foolish man I was to come out here, trying to be the law in this . . . this. . . ."

"Barbaric land?"

"No, not barbaric, just different. In the East we gather clues, evidences, write summons and only then move with force."

Randlett felt better about including Draper. The Sheriff had a right to ride posse and Randlett actually wanted the law if things worked out as he planned. "Okay, here's what will happen." Randlett took a piece of paper and began to draw the stage road, explaining how the hills sheltered the area before the Pass, how the previous robberies took place at the same spot for the good reason of cover and retreat areas to the north.

"Our three horses will be waiting east of this hold-up spot. Coming in from the north, the gang—and there should be four if Simon is with them—will not see us. We'll jump in before they can draw a gun. "How good are you with a long gun, Draper? Ever killed a man?"

Draper looked down at his twirling pencil and shook his head.

Randlett slapped his hat against his boot. "Okay, you practice between now and Wednesday. And if you're not sleeping well get Doc to fix you a tonic. You'll need a steady hand to hit a gun-slinging killer who suddenly finds himself cornered."

Sheriff Draper took a long breath and turned white.

Randlett shoved his hat on and left hoping he hadn't been a fool to give Will Draper his chance.

Abigail McMillan enjoyed going to Conger. Her Aunt Pearl was a happy, buxom woman who loved to mother her only niece. She lived in a twenty room house with a garden of flowers crowding the front in place of a yard. She kept two maids and a gardener busy at all times.

Without chores to do Abby had leisure to spare. She shopped but only came away with two dresses, a long winter cape, and some boots. She supposed one of the dresses would do to be married in but somehow the thrill of preparing for her marriage was not what she'd expected. Probably the heat, she told herself.

The second morning she went to see Mr. James Lankford at the bank. She had a letter from her father to withdraw money from their savings. For a fence her father had said. She could not understand these sudden plans to improve the ranch, and all this money he wanted sent back was going to be a great chunk out of their savings. Maybe it was really a wedding gift, she reasoned, and found herself not particularly elated at the thought. The money should be used for the ranch as they'd always planned. Suddenly she wanted to be home.

"Your father wants to hire a couple of men to ride back with this money, Miss McMillan," Lankford explained as he read the letter. "I'll have men and the stage ready before daylight. Will you be staying long with us in Conger?"

"A few more days," Abby said but as she walked out of the bank she changed her mind. One more day in town would be too long.

Of course Aunt Pearl would never agree to her going

back so soon. But she would leave a note with an invitation for her aunt to come to Wolfe City immediately to oversee the wedding. That would delight her aunt so that she'd forget about the quick get-away.

She could barely sit that evening with her aunt to discuss the details of the cake, of the preacher, of the flowers, of the punch . . . would it be with whiskey or not? All she could think of was the ranch with the long cool stretch of grassland surrounding it and the mountains seen from her window in the early morning sun. Oh, Suede, she cried to herself, how can I possibly leave the ranch and live in St. Louis?

The horses hitched to the coach were feisty, ready to go the next morning. Dark hovered over Conger, but the two men chosen to escort her father's money were working quickly and deftly without light. Suddenly Abby appeared in front of the stage.

"I've decided to go back to the ranch, Mr. Timms. You don't mind a passenger do you?" She expected a hearty " 'wall shore, ma'am'." Instead the two men glanced at each other and Timms said, "We'd like nothing better, ma'am, but we have strict orders about this shipment. We take only this money . . . that's all. You understand how yore pa is, don't chu, miss?"

"Yes," she said with a pang of disappointment. "I decided just last night that I really need to be back home . . . sure you can't let me ride?"

Both shook their heads. "Orders can't be broke this time, Miss McMillan. We'd be in mighty big trouble both with the sheriff and with yore pa."

Abby stepped back and nodded as if agreeing, but her mind was spinning. It was absurd that she shouldn't be allowed to ride on the stage especially hired by her father to go directly to the ranch. If her father were here he'd say yes.

She walked quietly up to the servant who stood by her boxes. "Take these back to my aunt's house, Todd. And don't say anything to her. I've left a note that explains everything."

She grabbed a medium portmanteau that held a change of clothes and a few of the things she'd bought for her trousseau and quietly waited until the old servant drove away in the buggy.

The two drivers had forgotten her as they tended to the harness, arguing over who would ride shotgun or who would drive. They were loading a box of food onto the floor under the seat and busily breaking out a chew when Abby opened the opposite door and slipped up into the coach.

The men boarded the outside seat, clucked to the team and headed for Wolfe City.

Abby settled back, heaving a sigh of satisfaction at her small deception.

Chapter Twenty-one

Randlett and Draper were joined at the fork near the end of town by a stout, pesky buckskin and rider. When Draper saw who the third man was, he jerked a look at Randlett. Then with a shake of his head he moved to the other side of the road to allow room for Tom Stalking Deer.

Well, Randlett thought, the good sheriff was really going to let him run the show . . . and without question it seemed. Who would have believed it?

The three-man posse traveled steadily west. The hot morning sun sweat-soaked each of their backs. No one spoke.

They rode without a break until mid afternoon when they pulled off into a cedar thicket. They were now just east of the Big Rock boulders where they expected the Fetty gang to hide.

Excitement churned Randlett's stomach as he dismounted behind the low-growing grove of cedars.

At a look from Stalking Deer Randlett whispered,

"McMillan says the stage should be here 'bout sunset. There could be four in Fetty's gang . . . if Simon is with them. Remember we hope to catch them before they even reach the stage . . . between the two Big Rocks . . . so follow my lead. When I ride out, flank me close enough to let them know we mean business."

Stalking Deer grunted and Draper wiped his brow. The sheriff held a .44 rifle dangling in his left hand as if it were a snake and might wiggle loose any minute. "Don't shoot the kid, Draper, whatever you do," Randlett could not help growling.

The grey was jittery, receiving a message from Randlett as he eased into the saddle. Like a brilliant ball of fire the sun sat right in the middle of the road and Randlett knew they'd never be able to see the stage if it came within the next few minutes. His neck ached and he suddenly felt this was going to be a mistake.

"I'm riding ahead," he told Draper and Stalking Deer. "I'll still be east, but behind the first big Rock. Be ready when I give a yell."

In a soft-footed dash he urged the grey around the curve and slipped behind a clump of trees. He stopped, listened for the rattle of the stage or creak of leather saddles. Nothing. Damn! Where was Fetty? Randlett should now be able to see the gang if they were hidden where they should be.

Then he heard it . . . the stage was crossing the pass. The last blinding rays of the sun struck Randlett just as he heard the heart-stopping sound of a whinnying horse and the racketing blast of gunfire. Not from this side of the boulder but west of it! Fetty had changed his tactic! The fiend was tackling the stage before the Rocks.

With a pain in his chest sharp as a knife Randlett gigged the gelding out of hiding and around the boulder.

He was joined by Draper and Stalking Deer and they tore down the sun-drenched road at a hard gallop.

West of the rocks was an eternity away. Randlett prayed they'd not be too late.

A swirl of blinding confusion greeted them. The driver of the coach was already down—shot through the head, his body flopping between the hooves of the frantic horses whose lines were held by another of the raiders. That pip-squeak, Bugs Harper. The other deputy began to fire from his perch atop the stage but as he stood up to aim he was pelted from the side by a second bandit.

Randlett was not close enough for a shot and Draper and Stalking Deer could see only shadows and flashes of light.

As the grey skidded to a stop fifty feet from the racketing coach, Randlett took aim at the robber holding the reins—this was the old man, Soda McPherson. Randlett fired two shots, missed with one and winged the geezer with the second. The man whirled his mount around and headed north at a dust-banging Hi!

In the muffled distance Randlett heard the rifles of his own men. Then they were beside him, firing shots that dusted the ground under the midget gunman, Harper, who also decided against continuing the game. Dancing to one side he took a single far-flung shot and headed after his companion.

Quickly Randlett turned the grey to go around the stage horses and saw a third bandit pull open the door of the coach. Then a scream rent the air. A woman's scream. The scream of Abby McMillan. Randlett couldn't believe it but somehow Abby McMillan was inside that stage.

Randlett swore. He could never reach her in time.

Then he saw a red headband and flash of wild pony

as Stalking Deer came in from the other side firing his Winchester. The Indian's shot missed but the gunman was rattled. He turned, his own rifle flaring red with a single shot that knocked Stalking Deer out of the saddle.

Randlett kneed the grey toward the bandit and sent a flurry of wild shots that blew off his hat. But the man was already mounted and pivoting his horse in a ninety degree turn, racing for open country.

The door of the carriage was open. Randlett swung off and scrambled to peer inside, his gun drawn. It was Abby. She sat crouched in one corner, her eyes uncannily vacant and staring. As he watched, her mouth contorted into a long nerve-shattering wail.

Randlett instantly decided she was unmarked. She was terrified but not hurt.

He left the coach and ran to the fallen Indian, dropping to his knees beside him. Stalking Deer had not moved since he fell. Randlett felt a wave of nausea sweep over him. He closed his eyes. When the sickness passed he was looking down at the lifeless body of his friend.

Tentatively he reached out to touch the Indian's smooth young face. Randlett's whole frame shuddered. Bitter tears stung his eyes, pooled there in anguish and finally spilled over to course like a firebrand down his cheeks.

He sat for a long moment not hearing the fearful screams of Abby McMillan.

Finally, rising on one knee, he turned to find Draper. The Sheriff was stumbling toward the two hired men lying in the road. He gave them a quick look then slumped onto his knees where he sat staring into space.

Randlett holstered his gun and climbed into the stage. Abby's screams had changed to hysterical sobbing. He raised her up by the waist and set her down outside the coach. She fell against him and he held her there until her sobs grew slower. When they settled into a sickening moan he still held her but with one eye now on Draper who had fallen over in the sandy road. Was he dead too?

Stroking the long unbound tresses of the frightened girl Randlett felt a chill course down his spine. He gazed alternately at the body of his friend, Tom Stalking Deer, then at the two stricken drivers and at the still form of Sheriff Draper. What had happened? Was that Fetty on the red horse? Where was Simon?

Oh, Lord! What had he done?

Chapter Twenty-two

Randlett had two helpless, distraught people on his hands. Draper was not dead . . . he was not even wounded. But he was so rattled he was speechless and had to be led off the road.

Pushing his thoughts and feelings into the back of his mind, Randlett began to do what was necessary. Before darkness blanketed the narrow aisle between the peaks he untangled the lines and unhitched the team. He gathered the reins and led the whole crew, including their own horses, into a stand of trees. He picketed them to graze, then began to gather wood for a fire.

Abby stood obediently near the flames, her hunched shoulders jerking in short, hard spasms.

From his pack Randlett extracted a sack of coffee. He threw a double fistful of grounds into the pot and filled it with water from his canteen.

Standing in a trance, he waited for it to boil. When it was ready he handed a scalding cup to the sheriff. Draper was shaky, unable to move. He sat on a fallen log where

Randlett had left him. But he took the cup, smothering it in both hands, bending his head down over the steaming contents. He drank in gulps, choking on every other swallow.

Randlett let Abby drink while he held the cup—the girl was too distressed to handle it herself.

Tramping in a circle, Randlett found a mass of tall grass in a gully. He pulled several armloads and carrying them back to the fire, piled them beside a slanted rock. Over the grass he laid a slicker and blanket from the back of Draper's mount. Coaxing her as he would a child, he led the dazed girl over and she fell onto the bed, flinging an arm over her face.

Next he laid out a blanket and saddle for Draper close to the pile of tree limbs he had gathered. Taking the empty cup from Draper's clenched hand, Randlett spoke harshly, "Sheriff, keep the fire going! You understand? Don't let it die out."

He left Draper hugging himself, glaring at the wood.

Feet heavy with unutterable despair, Randlett went to bury the men.

At the road's edge he paused to gain strength. A fist twisted his insides as he bent over Stalking Deer. The body was cold, already stiff. Randlett found it difficult to breathe. He shook his head. The bullet had struck the Indian center-chest, the wound had sealed over, virtually no blood was lost. Randlett smiled fleetingly as he pulled off the magic red headband and stuffed it in his shirt front.

Suddenly the idea of what he wanted to do with his friend came to him . . . and with it a burst of energy. Rolling Stalking Deer onto a wool blanket he found tied behind the buckskin, he rolled the body and blanket up together. Then he wound a rope in a spiral the entire length and tied it.

He hefted the wrapped figure over his back, then onto the back of the short buckskin pony. Drawing the horse into a grove of tall oaks north of the road, he heaved the body into a fork of one of the ancients. It was high enough to be protected from predators . . . at least until he returned.

He murmured some Cheyenne words and went back to the stage.

Pent-up heat shimmered off the road, sapping Randlett's new-found strength. He felt as if he could lie down and never get up. Forcing his legs to move, he staggered under the load, but managed to drag the hired deputies off onto a sand bar. Using his knife he dug a shallow trench and toppled the two men into it. He piled rocks over the sand. If men from Wolfe City wanted to rebury them, so be it.

The money was in a steel box inside the coach. The box was small and it contained paper money so that it weighed only ten pounds. Randlett carried it to the boulders behind the peak and secured it in a crevice. Brushing away his boot prints, he returned to the fire.

It was dusk. Abby was asleep, her breathing gentle and slow. He drew the blanket over her feet.

The fire had died and he tossed several large limbs on, then dragged his own saddle near Draper. The sheriff was lying down, his bloodshot eyes staring into the fire.

"Go to sleep, Draper," Randlett advised gruffly. "Tomorrow we're going after them." Randlett knew how the man felt. He blamed himself. At the same time he was frightened to his toenails.

"I'm going to need your help again, so rest up." Randlett turned over and was asleep in seconds.

Draper was the one to rise first out of their dew-damp beds. He had regained some of his nerve though his hands still shook. He took the horses to a stream and back, then saddled his mare and the grey.

Randlett roused, his body stiff with yesterday's fatigue. He looked over at the girl. She still slept. He got up and made fresh coffee then dug biscuits and dry fruit from his pack. When he took food over to Abby she sat up instantly, her eyes bright with memories of the past night.

"Eat this, then get ready for a few hours wait." Randlett set the tin plate on the ground then stood over her and drank his coffee. "Someone will be along later in the day on the road. The regular stage should be in today too. I'll leave a flag out there and a note, but you can hail them down yourself."

"Wh . . . what are you going to do?"

"I'm going to get Fetty, Miss McMillan, and I'll not be coming back until I do. You tell your father what happened . . . I hate to put this on you but there's no other way. I'll show you where I've hidden the money."

Her gold-blue eyes blinked hard, her body trembled. She clasped her arms around her doubled-up legs and buried her face against her knees. Her words were choked. "It was Suede, Mr. Randlett. Opening the door of the coach and . . . and looking in."

She broke into a deep sob and lowered her face again into her folded arms.

Randlett sputtered his coffee into the dirt. "Suede? Are you sure? It wasn't someone you didn't know?"

Her head shot up. "No. It was Suede. Or Simon. Oh, heaven help me, he must be your brother . . . did you see him?"

"The sun was in my eyes. He was just a figure against

the sun. He turned and shot St. . . ." Randlett couldn't finish.

Abby nervously stated, "You were right, Mr. Randlett, he must be with those men. And I did recognize one of the others. I was looking out the window on the other side and saw that old man who was at the dance . . . the one who kept watching Simon."

"Soda McPherson," Draper said as he walked up. "Right, Randlett?'

"Yes, that's him." Randlett sat down on Draper's log and wiped his face with his handkerchief. "If that was Simon then Fetty was not even there. Why not? Did I hurt him so bad he can't ride? Or is he forcing Simon to take his place just out of devilment. . . . Abby, did he say anything to you . . . did he look frightened . . . or. . . ."

"No," she whispered, "he just looked surprised. He was simply surprised." She put her face into her hands and shuddered.

Randlett stood up and waving his empty coffee cup at Draper said, "Mount up, sheriff, we're headin' out."

Abby McMillan lurched drunkenly to her feet and followed. "Mr. Randlett," her voice was different, clear, frantically energetic. "I'm a fair shot with a rifle and you can use me . . . I'm going with you."

Randlett turned. "Nothing doing, Miss McMillan, your pa will be upset enough as it is. What in tarnation were you doing on that stage anyway?"

"I was going home! You all evidently thought you couldn't trust me and so your little trick backfired." She nearly broke but she bit her bottom lip and added, "It was your idea wasn't it . . . to . . . to trap Suede."

"To trap Fetty, Miss McMillan, in order to get Simon away from his clutches."

"What if . . . what if Simon is actually doing this because he wants to."

"We have no evidence of that," Randlett said. "He shot Stalking Deer out of sheer self defense. And as for the money, well. . . ."

"I want to find out about Suede as much as you do, Mr. Randlett. I'm going if I have to walk every step of the way." She glanced at the bulky ring on her finger and Randlett knew he couldn't stop her.

"It'll be hot."

"I know."

"You'll get hungry."

"Yes."

"You may not like what we find and we may all be killed."

"Yes, I know. But I'm going."

"Then leave a note for your father."

Chapter Twenty-three

Abby rode Stalking Deer's buckskin. Her portmanteau contained a pair of riding pants, some extra linen, and several new things she'd bought in Conger. Randlett made her change into the pants then he stuffed the rest into a pouch slung over the pony. It would be cold as they climbed into the Fox Tails and the extra clothes might be needed.

There were four canteens including the large one on the stage and Randlett filled them at the stream. There was only enough food for two or three days. They'd need to kill game to survive longer. And it would take longer.

Randlett did not try to spare Abby McMillan. Their lives depended upon getting to the outlaws before they had time to plan or heal. Draper was certain at least one had been hit.

By late afternoon they were deep in the canyons. Abby was drooping and red-faced but she gallantly urged the pony to keep up by a constant drumming of her heels.

Draper too was exhausted but he did not complain.

Randlett went the shortest way toward the same mountain area he'd been trapped in . . . where he had beat Fetty into unconsciousness. Maybe, it seemed, even killed the crook.

He read the sun to be about five o'clock when they reached a small dry box canyon. Heat on the floor was dreadful. Hipping around in the saddle, Randlett scowled at the girl. She wore one of the deputy's hats. It was too large and she kept pushing it up off her face. She carried one of their rifles across her saddle, shifting it every few minutes to ease her cramped arms.

Sweat poured from their faces and they craved water. They had already used up the canteens. Randlett had made them drink as much as they could from the first few hours. "Saving water to dribble out a little at a time is not the way to survive. Saturate your body as soon as you can, you'll last longer," he advised.

As the passageway widened, a reef of slate stuck out sharply from one side of the arroyo. Deep under its wings was enough space for them to camp, for the horses to hide and for them to make a fire.

Randlett gave Abby and Draper tasks to perform then he took off on foot to find water.

Away from human sound he forgot about danger. His taut muscles relaxed. The sounds and smells of the earth came vividly to him, soothing his tortured nerves. Humans fouled up, got hurt . . . died. But the earth and its own remained constant, always renewing itself and whoever partook from it.

Vegetation was sparse. Rainfall was nonexistent in these canyons. But he knew underground streams, waterfalls, or seeps could appear suddenly in barren rockbed.

He began to walk in a circular pattern, hunting for

signs. He trouped over boulders, ridges and knolls until pink touched the western sky. Then there! He picked up a well-worn deer trail. He turned down it, followed it across a pallet of feathered bunchgrass to a slight dip where another path joined it. This was an old wolf trail and he smiled knowing he was close to water.

The pool lay deep behind a cleft of sandstone. Huge white boulders tumbled around the basin preventing it from being seen. The edge on one slope was worn where the animals had come to drink. He filled the canteens then drank his fill.

It took less than ten minutes to return to camp and he and Draper brought the horses back to drink. He dared not camp at the water hole. He wanted to hide his fire and besides, others might know of the hole. They were bordering Indian country now.

No one wanted hot food—Draper and Abby were sick-tired. They chewed on jerky and biscuits then drank hot coffee and huddled close to the fire. Night was cold in the canyons.

Draper and Abby were asleep as soon as they lay down. But Randlett sat staring at the fire, wondering how they would get past the Blackfeet near the mesa if they did not come upon the outlaw trio before then. No plan came to him.

The next day they traveled silently throughout the morning. The canyon floor lifted out into a swale of ground covered by stubby dry weeds. Randlett could see the plateau that began the climb into the mountains.

They rested in the late afternoon. Abby was blistered, her lips peeling and dark freckles had popped out across her nose. Her shirt was torn and her arm scratched. She swigged a slow drink from the canteen. "Oh, I never knew water could taste so good. You know," she sighed, her voice low and husky, "you were right at the dance. I did think you were Simon when you came up on me and called my name. But . . . I also thought there was something . . . something about you that I knew, or . . . or loved the first time I bumped into you on the boardwalk." Her eyes darted away but she continued. "I thought it was because of Simon that I always got a funny feeling around you. Now . . ." she picked at a twig of dry grass and seemed unable to finish.

"Now what?" Randlett asked, his own voice suddenly dry.

"Now, I think I saw in you the man that Simon could . . . or should be."

Randlett leaned back, his eyes closed. They stung, prickly under tight lids. When he turned toward her she held out the ring. "Here, it's not mine. It means nothing to me any more." She dropped it into his palm.

When Randlett hesitated she said, "It belongs to you." Then evidently trying to lighten the mood she asked, "What was it your father wanted you to do when he gave it to you? You mentioned something about the hidden heirlooms."

"Huh!" Randlett scoffed. "I don't know. That's the trouble. Maybe he was trying to tell me about the jewels and the money but I've never been able to remember what he was saying."

"Try," she said as if he had never really done so. "It's in your memory somewhere, just relax and try to think."

"Well, he kept saying 'turn left, twice' . . . I do remember that much. But there were no roads where we were or had been. We were following a wagon trail and that mostly by general directions."

Abby squinted. "But he must have thought you would know or he wouldn't have said such a thing."

They both settled back to doze and think their own thoughts.

Then Abby was sitting up. "Maybe he meant turn *it* left, twice." She reached for the ring and when Randlett gave it to her she began pressing, struggling to turn the huge initial set inside the gold circle. When she finally grasped the right side and pushed on the big R at the top it moved. Holding her breath she turned it all the way around, then again. And the engraving popped open to reveal a small treasure box.

She squealed with delight. "Kane, look!" she cried and Randlett realized she was using his first name . . . for the first time. He scooted close and stared at the ring. "Thunder! Anything in that little box?" His heart was thudding fiercely in his chest and he barely caught the tiny fold of paper that fell out. It was tightly rolled and his one hand could not manipulate it. Abby took it, opened it into a one inch square.

"It's a picture." They studied the tiny image that resembled the top of a rabbit's head, his two ears upright. A mark behind one of them. At the bottom written in script so small they could barely make it out were the words: '1 mi. w. Valleyview'.

"That's a real place, Valleyview," Randlett said in a hush. "It's on the Whitehorse River. And that is not a rabbit it's two hills that we laughed about and called rabbit's ears. We stopped there for two nights." Randlett smiled, nodding, remembering.

"Then that mark must be where your father buried your family's money," Abby concluded. Her eyes sparked at the wonder of it but Randlett felt a loosening within his chest not unlike regret. This was what Simon had needed to be free of that menace, Leek Fetty. Well, maybe it was not too late. Maybe there would still be time to buy Simon's freedom.

"What did your family have, Kane, that was so precious?"

"Well, for one thing there was a sack of gold coins, don't know how much but pa wanted to open a school . . . said he could do it. As for jewels my mother had some from her family. I remember a comb that she particularly liked. It was silver studded with some sort of blue and green stones." He glanced at the mass of ash blond hair that sat atop Abby's head, it's unruly curls escaping down the back of her neck. "It would go right nice with your eyes and hair, Miss McMillan."

"Abby," she said slowly in a whisper. Awkardly fussing with her shirt she stood up.

"Yes," he agreed, "let's get going. Draper, mount up!"

As Randlett gathered the reins of the grey a shot careened out of the rocks. He saw Abby from the corner of his eye as she flung the rifle to one side and fell free of the buckskin.

Randlett dropped to his knees, his gun palmed. "Draper!" he commanded. "Atop that ledge, sun-side!"

A figure darted over the ridge two hundred yards away and the sheriff fired. A volley answered, driving Draper back under the rocks. He poked his head out and fired again only to receive another round that brought a curdled cry from his throat.

Randlett heard him curse as he fell on his face.

Frantic—too far away for a pistol shot—Randlett looked for Abby and when he saw her he rolled over and swooping her up, forced her to run to a slit in the boulder opposite Draper. A slug tore off his hat in the process.

A man stood up on the promontory. "Give it up, Randlett!" called the gravelly-voiced Bugs Harper. "Your only rifle is out. You ain't got a chance. The kid's gone on to the Nest with Soda so you and me are it and I aim to kill the girl. And you too this time."

Randlett pushed Abby further into the crack. Nodding at the rifle on the ground nearby he asked, "Draper's hit. You say you can use that?"

Her head shook. "Is there just one of them out there?" She took the rifle and steadying her eye along the barrel propped it against the rockface.

"Looks like it as far as I can tell. Evidently it was old McPherson who got hit." Randlett's eyes drew to a thin slit. He licked the salt off his lips. "Shoot a path for me. Just don't aim too low."

She fired quickly, expertly. Randlett grinned as he scooted catlike from rock to rock around the ledge where Harper hid.

Diving behind a lowslung outcrop Randlett drilled three quick slugs into Harper's lair. He saw the outlaw flinch, heard him curse.

Harper was leveling the rifle when two shots zinged past his head from the rocks where Abby fired. He twisted, fired, and took a hard drag on his cigarette, trying to figure which rock Randlett was behind now.

"Here, Harper!" Randlett called, then hunching over he sidled out to crouch behind another boulder.

Bugs Harper stepped out of his hiding place firing in three directions, mad with confusion.

Randlett crabbed into the open not twenty feet from the outlaw. Elated, Harper jerked up the Winchester but he was too close. Randlett shot from the hip, cutting the bantam gunman in two across the chest.

Chapter Twenty-four

Draper lay deathly still. Hunkering beside his head, Randlett put his hand on the Sheriff's chest. Unconscious but alive. His leg was bloody and when Randlett slit the pants he found a hole welling with blood.

Abby was instantly there pulling her bandana around Draper's lower thigh. Without a comment she put a stick into a knot and began to twist until the blood stopped.

"Let's get him into the shade . . . there, behind those ledges," Randlett said.

When they had pulled Draper under the lee of the rocks Abby examined the wound. "The flesh is torn but it looks like the bullet went all the way through. Let's pray he doesn't bleed to death. Kane, bring me my bundle. I have something in it that will help." Her gaze shifted to rest on the dead buckskin. She winced, then dropped her head to loosen the tourniquet.

Dumping her belongings upside down on the hard earth Randlett rummaged through the clothes. "What is it you want, bandage?"

"No. There's a small bottle wrapped in . . . in one of those white things. Bring it here."

He unrolled a soft lacy creation—an undergarment no doubt—and Randlett touched it gingerly with thumb and finger. The bottle was square, made of dark brown glass. Frowning, he read the label: Dr. Simmons' Liver Regulator.

"That should do nicely to prevent infection," she said and reached for the medicine. She uncorked the bottle and poured the liquid directly into the open hole on the Sheriff's leg. He thrashed about then groaning, lay still. "Aunt Pearl sends Dad a bottle of this every month," Abby explained. "I know there's nothing wrong with him so I suspect the alcohol content is the draw."

Deftly easing the deep wound together she bandaged it tightly with the Sheriff's own handkerchief. Then she sat back on her heels and asked, "Are we safe?"

"Looks like it. Harper said he was alone and that's probably the only truth he ever told."

"What do we do now?"

"Rest and watch. Get ready to tackle the Fox Tails. Unless I can persuade you to stay with Draper here. Seems you know a bit about nursing."

Draper roused and wobbling his head from side to side in pain grunted, "Take her, Randlett. You'll need a rifle and she can shoot. I'll . . . I'll be okay. Just leave me a gun." He closed his eyes so tightly they watered, then he slumped into a fitful sleep.

"I'll build a fire," was Randlett's comment.

By nightfall they had made a soup from dried jerky and a single potato. They drank a pot of coffee then Abby rolled into her blanket and was asleep.

On the promontory where the outlaw's body still lay in the open, Randlett squatted against a boulder and studied the north passage. The odds of the chase have changed, Randlett thought with a flicker of fear. The danger is greater. Two outlaws remain . . . one hurt badly but still able to spread his venom, the other also wounded. Then there is Simon. And now they must figure in the Indians.

Randlett's mind raced. He had another twenty four hours to come up with a plan but he still had no idea how to deal with the feckless, unpredictable band of Blood that guarded the mesa. They were like spoiled children yet the results of an encounter with them was no child's play. Killing was simply a matter of getting what they wanted.

In the quiet before dawn the sound of footsteps drew him up sharply. Abby McMillan came up the hill and leaned beside him against the rocky cliff. She held her rifle. "You think some of them will try again?'

"No. Not the gang. We're at the edge of Blackfeet territory, Abby. We have a new worry now."

Her eyes keened to a sharp pinpoint as she scanned the peaks before them.

"Draper okay?" he asked.

"Yes. I got some of Dr. Simmons' Liver Tonic down him. He should sleep for several more hours. Why don't you get some rest. I'll watch."

"No, I'll make it," he said firmly.

"What are you afraid of, Kane? Do Cheyenne women never fight?"

Randlett studied the frail-looking girl. In the hazy light of the predawn her white skin held a pearly sheen. Her arms and neck were velvety smooth, the bones underneath her face soft and rounded and vulnerable . . . able to support her small body but not substantial enough to fight a hostile world. How could she survive what must come?

Waiting for his answer her slim fingers clenched the barrel of the rifle.

Randlett noticed the upward tilt of her chin, the defiant gleam in her intelligent eye. "No, Abby," he finally said, "Cheyenne women do not fight in battle with guns and tomahawks. They're given the 'lesser' task of burying the braves and carrying on alone the rest of their lives."

Pushing himself away from the cliff he added, "You watch then."

Her eyes widened in solemn anticipation and Randlett left, praying that Pat McMillan would understand what his daughter was doing . . . and why.

They reached the pines bordering the mountains by late afternoon the next day. They had left Draper with all the food and three of the canteens. He had waved them good-bye with his rifle, insisting he would be there when they returned.

That man's grown a bit, Randlett mused. The Sheriff was turning out to be a man to have beside you, a man who did not complain, a man who could relieve the task of decision-making by accepting the less glorious job of staying behind and waiting.

Abby was riding Draper's big black, now fidgety and lathered to a foam. Randlett thought she must be sore in every muscle but there was no holding her back. She had cried herself to sleep last night and now he could sense her fear, the terror that had begun to build knowing they were soon riding into the enemy camp.

So far they'd not seen any Indians. But that simply meant they were not visible.

Crossing the Bitter Weed Divide had been pure torture. Every nerve was a-tingle and his head ached with the strain of staying alert, ready to ride, or drop into the weeds in case of attack. Why hadn't they been beset by one of those wild bands of lawless braves hunting a coup? Were they waiting to get them inside their camp? Had Fetty prepared for such a thing?

Then as they clambered into the first peaks of the Fox Tails he had been able to relax in the saddle. In the mountains they would stop one more time before he must decide a strategy for braving the huts of old Chief Red Vest.

They made that last stop at the end of another day atop the last of the peaks that bounded the plain claimed by the Indians.

Randlett had killed a prairie hen while crossing the Bitter Weed and by sheer luck he had shot a small mountain goat when they climbed the first peak. He had cut off the hams and now they roasted those and hungrily ate them with a sprinkling of salt he always carried.

It was an uneasy night on the windy mountain. Their clothes were damp from the sweat of the day and they shivered beside the fire. Randlett had decided to chance a fire. The Indians already knew they were coming. This was their territory.

He sat on his heels away from the flame, his eyes piercing the darkness, his ears attune for strange noises. How he wished Lon were with him. Instead he had the task of protecting this frail girl from harm. Impossible, he told himself. And tomorrow when we go down into that plain . . . what will happen? What will I say or do? A hard knot jammed against his ribs and he felt as if he would choke.

Abby began to hum and he turned and watched her slim form as she moved about near the fire. He watched her pull a long grey cloak from her pouch and throwing it around her shoulders hunch into its warm folds. It was grey, he had seen it when he had looked for the tonic.

Randlett sat up. He remembered something else about that cape. "Yes!" he said aloud as the idea came to him. He smiled and that knot in his chest loosened itself out. He knew how they would gain entrance to the camp of the aging chief!

"Abby," he said, energy coursing through his veins, "let me see that cape."

Abby stood unresponsive as he lifted one end and studied the lining. He whooped and threw his fist into the air. "I was right, look!" And he turned up the corner for her to see.

When she did not respond he said, "See how it shines . . . see that glorious blood-red shine?"

"It's satin, Kane. Crimson satin. Yes, it is nice."

"Not nice, Abby. Its our ticket. That cloak is going to get us into the exalted presence of the chief of the Blood Clan of the Blackfeet.

He picked up her bundle and tossed it upside down as he had before. Rummaging through the soft undergarments he plucked out two muffs of snow-white ermine. He held them up and said, "Abby, help me attach these to the collar of that cape."

"I . . . I don't have any thread or needle," she began in consternation.

"Then here." He reached toward his saddle lying on the ground and plucked off four strips of piggin' string from the edge of the lower flaps. He handed them to her. "And make the fur visible from the inside."

When she began to shake her head he said, "The old Chief craves showy white men's garments . . . he has a red vest right now that he loves so much he wears it all the time and even named himself after it . . . Chief Red

Vest. Maybe he'll crave a magnificent red satin cape with a white ermine collar."

"Yes," she said with a smile creeping over her lips and she set to work.

Chapter Twenty-five

The night's sleep was a restless one for both of them. In the early dawn Abby was up poking sticks on the dying fire when Randlett returned from saddling their mounts. He had found a tin of raisins in Draper's saddle pack and they feasted on the sweet chewy gems with grins lighting their faces.

"You really believe this will work?" she asked.

"Can only hope," he answered. "If we're met, keep still and don't panic whatever they do. They'll try to frighten you."

Her eyes swam with emotion. Fear, excitement, anger! "You can still wait here, Abby," he said.

She jumped up and began to tighten the strings on the fur collar of the long heavy cape.

Randlett sighed and began to unlace his shirt. Hurriedly he stripped it off, then removed his boots and replaced them with low moccasins. When Abby looked up he stood clothed only in the tight deerskin pants and mocs. His body was darkly tanned and as he wrapped

Stalking Deer's headband around his head he changed into a Indian.

Abby did not notice the side of his body that had no arm. She could only stare at the good arm, its brown symmetry and rippling muscles marred . . . or graced, she did not know which . . . by a line of deep scars inside his forearm.

Randlett saw her question and he explained, "Cheyenne cut themselves when they mourn the death of a loved one. When we were sixteen, Stalking Deer and I had a friend who was killed by white trappers. We mourned together, as brothers, by cutting our arms in the same way."

Abby was silent as she handed him the cloak. She watched him swirl it up and around his shoulders. Then he motioned for her to tie the neck strap. "Hot as Hades, but let's hope it does the trick," he commented and throwing a salute, jumped on the grey.

Randlett looked neither right nor left as he led the way down into the low plain leading to Dripping Springs. He held his head high and straight and rode as if he knew where he was going and that he had a right to go there. The crimson cloak shining against the long rays of the morning sun, and the snow-white collar and regal band around his head gave him the look of a storybook king riding off to war.

In truth he was damnably hot. A deep, paralyzing heat inside the cape made him yearn to claw it off. The fur itched his neck. He desperately wanted to sneeze.

But it was working!

For an hour they had been closely watched, followed, yet no one threatened.

Birds chirped in the needles under the pines as they rode through the last stand of trees. Overhead a carrion bird floated listlessly. Randlett heard no human sound but he could feel the presence of hostile eyes as they reached the plateau. Before them laid out in a mile circle, were the hide lodges of the Blackfeet.

The grey snorted and Randlett could smell them too: the rank odor of rancid bear fat on unwashed flesh. He stopped. Her eyes dancing with fear, Abby brought the mare close. Then suddenly they were surrounded by naked bodies and staring black eyes.

There were ten warriors in all. Two or three were old with straggly hair and haggard faces. But the others were young with streaks of yellow and white paint down their noses and across their cheeks. Ready to count coup!

One, on a small pinto pony, brandished a long spear, its tip fashioned from the broken blade of a knife. Without warning he lunged across his mount, jabbing the lance at Randlett's body. Randlett jerked back, the grey sidestepping.

The spear was deflected downward but its point ripped the rawhide along his thigh. Teeth gritted in a snarl, Randlett flung a command to Abby, "Stay quiet. No matter what happens, don't interfere."

He did not look at his leg but he knew it was bleeding. A gush of liquid, hot and sticky seeped down his leg. It burned like a fire-hot branding iron.

Clucking to the grey, Randlett fought to keep him steady among the milling circle of ponies. Glaring at first one and then another of the nearest braves, he began a tirade in Cheyenne. Evidently they understood enough of the tongue—or maybe it was the chilling tone of the words—for they quietened and stared fixedly at him.

As they held a truce, mounts nosing and pawing the earth, Randlett explained to Abby in a level, emotionless tone, "I've told them I am an important White Chief.

That I'm wearing the band of Tom Stalking Deer because the bandits hiding in their mountain mesa have killed him. I've asked to see their Chief. And I said his name."

In the front line an argument broke out between a crooked-nosed youth and an old warrior. They each spat out a barrage of anger, pointing, gesturing, trying unsuccessfully to push the other's horse back into the group.

From the other side another young buck jostled through on a tall bay gelding. Grinning wickedly he yelled, "Hiyeeeee!" and slapped Abby's mare on the rump, sending her into a frightened gallop. The buck took pursuit, laughing and shouting.

Randlett could hear Abby's calls to the mare as she fought to stay in the saddle. He cringed, his stomach tightening into fighting rage. But he knew one thing. He could not condescend to fight. Not now. Not for a "squaw". His only chance was the power of the cape and the childish awe and fear of authority it might wield over these people.

He kicked the grey forward, riding straight ahead, eyes never leaving the center lodge of the Indian camp that spread out before them half a mile away.

When Abby's single, high-pitched scream tore across the plain Randlett ached to turn, to draw the Colt and blast that young hooligan off his charging pony. But he held tight, forcing himself not to think what the creature was doing to her. He had to believe the rambunctious braves would not go too far without their Chief's authority. He had to believe it.

The other braves hedged him in, their ponies crowding against the grey. They jeered and talked, pointed to his headband, argued among themselves. Then four broke away to race at breakneck speed, vying for one another's attention by performing tricks. They hung off the sides and back and front of their steeds. They touched the ground with hand or toe then leaped back into the saddle. One stood on the rump of his mount, hands aloft in a salute of triumph.

Randlett noticed Abby and her captor were at a standstill, watching, the young upstart gesturing first to Abby and then at his friends' antics. Then the shouts and laughter of Abby's tormentor sailed over the grass and brought the sweat pouring from Randlett's face. He dared a look and saw Abby swatted with a backhand as she rode too close to the giggling Indian.

Randlett kept riding and finally the wild thumping of his heart slowed when he felt the mare ease up on his right flank. "You okay?" he asked in a low voice.

After a moment he heard a strangled, "Yes."

He knew it wasn't so but he pretended not to notice.

Head forward, coat flouncing behind, Randlett kneed the gelding down the incline into the camp.

He was shocked at the sight among the lodges. The place stank. Trash and bones and excrement littered the ground. The few pencil-legged children were runny-nosed and dirty. Offering toothless grins, a group of women turned an animal carcass on a spit. Randlett noted their bare arms and legs were covered with scabs from insect bites.

Half-way through the tents, a small boy ran out and stuck a long pole in front of Abby's black. The horse stumbled and Abby pitched onto the mare's neck, clinging with all her strength to stay upright. The boy laughed and ran.

Randlett caught the mare's halter and Abby sent him a sick smile. Her face was already turning blue on one side.

In front of the large center tent Randlett stopped. An old man stood in the doorway with his arms folded. He was grey-haired and tall. He wore a white man's western hat, a set of gold beads—gummy green and surely once belonging to a Madame—and a short breechclout. He had a fine Bowie knife holstered securely around a bulging stomach that in turn was too large for the tiny red vest that adorned it. He smoked a fancy black ebony pipe.

But his eye was on the cape as it had been for the last ten minutes . . . and Randlett smiled to himself.

In a guttural voice the old chief asked, "Do you know my name, one-arm of the Cheyenne?"

Randlett praised Stalking Deer for giving him that piece of information. "I know you are now called Chief Red Vest," he pronounced gravely.

The old man grunted and walked into the lodge.

Chapter Twenty-six

Randlett followed, with Abby at his heels.

The Chief squatted before a low fire and motioned Randlett to sit opposite. Randlett nodded for Abby to take her place at the rear of the huge tent, with a group of women and children who sat in total silence.

Using words of both tongues, and gestures coined by years of cultural contact, Randlett and Chief Red Vest talked. Once, when the children laughed the old man picked up a stick and threw it at them. A cowering four year old was knocked into silence. Abby sat beside the whimpering, runny-nosed child and frowned.

Suddenly Randlett addressed Abby without looking at her. "I've agreed, very reluctantly, to give him my cloak in exchange for safe passage through the Divide. He thinks I have special powers since I knew his latest name. Be ready to eat whatever they offer," he added as he took the bowl passed to him by one of the women. "It will seal our agreement."

Nodding slightly, he drank from the dish . . . his eyes

now lifted toward Abby. She smiled grimly, and as she accepted a bowl from one of the women Randlett's heart went out to her.

When she stared at the contents her face paled. She nearly dropped the bowl. She waited, still as a hunted rabbit, staring at the brew of bear fat soup swimming with little tendrils of bloody strings.

In panic she whipped her eyes toward Randlett. He merely took another sup from his own bowl then passed it to the chief.

The women waited, watching Abby. They stopped talking, did not move. Silently, Abby flung another silent plea toward Randlett. His answer was the grim closing of his eyes.

I can't do it, she cried to herself. Can't. Then she thought of Simon. Funny, she could no longer call him Suede. Suede was gone. The Suede she knew. But she had to find out why things were as they were . . . and who the young man really was she had promised to marry.

Eyes vacant, her thoughts a thousand miles away, she upped the bowl and let one of the globs slide down her throat.

Sweat stuck like glue to her forehead and she nearly gagged. But she cleared her throat and sat up straight. And smiled.

Outside the Chief's tent, the young buck who had harassed Abby waited with a sneer on his handsome face. Their mounts were gone and Randlett grabbed the rope-halter on the brave's pinto. The buck tried to jerk away but Randlett moved with him, his hold on the halter unbreakable.

Behind him Chief Red Vest spoke a command and the

hoodlum eased off, and in a moment had their horses back.

"He's a nasty one," Randlett said to Abby as he helped her into the saddle. "Don't leave my side." With an eye peeled for the movements of the young buck, Randlett gathered the reins of their mounts and weaved their way through the hogans to the outer edge of the encampment. They would stay the night before tackling Tepee Mesa.

Scissortails swooped daringly over the grassy field that stretched from the tents to the dark red outline of cliffs bordering this flat tableland on three sides. The fourth side opened to the low hills where Dripping Springs poured its fresh mountain water into a pool, where a mile further a tall earth mound rose out of the land, its sides perpendicular and unclimbable. The outlaw mesa called Tepee.

A chill ran down Randlett's neck as he thought of it. Tomorrow. One more day. One more twenty-four hour period to live through and he would be able to get to the boy. To come face to face with his brother.

How could he ever explain to Simon the feelings of guilt and frustration he had lived with all these years. Guilt at not being able to answer that wrenching cry for help the boy gave so long ago; frustration these last few weeks at not being able to fight the twisted maneuvering of Leek Fetty.

They had been offered a hogan at the far edge of the camp. Randlett accepted it for Abby's sake. After tossing out a pile of foul-smelling items he urged her inside to sleep. "I'll stay in the open," he told her, "so I can watch that buzzard who seems bent on tormenting you."

Abby's face was swollen, her eye nearly closed. "The Chief cannot control him?"

"Only by warnings. Those hooligans think its fun hurting someone. Sleep now."

Randlett turned toward the sunset. He studied the rising cliffs they must pass through in order to reach Dripping Springs and he could see no trail. Chief Red Vest promised an escort to the Springs but Randlett was leery of such an offer. He just hoped they lived through the night.

It was another tormenting night without sleep. He sat in a dugout burrow fifty feet in front of the tent where Abby evidently tossed and turned, making frightened noises and moans until deep into the night.

Randlett's leg ached and he wondered if it might be infected. As soon as he heard the stirrings of the camp . . . some woman making fire and slapping bread onto a hot rock . . . he rose and stretched.

His vigil had been for nothing. The braves had made noises drinking and laughing but had not ventured near Abby's tent.

The woman who made the bread came waddling over and set down a bowl of sticky porridge along with the flat cakes which ran with yellow honey. They accepted with thanks and happily made a feast of it.

Then the old chief came up riding a white bow-necked mustang. Red Vest's long hair was braided and he had stuck an eagle feather in it near the crown. He no longer wore the vest of his name but waited expectantly as Randlett stood up, offering him the grand red cape.

The cloak sat majestically on the tall old man and Abby thought it gave him a grand bearing. She hoped it also gave him power over his men. Several of those youngest braves now stamped their ponies impatiently waiting to lead them to the Divide.

At the Chief's signal the Indian escort broke into a

fast gallop toward the tow-sack colored hills encircling the camp. Abby's tormentor led the way.

The party pulled up at the base of the brown peaks at mid-morning. Randlett could see no way through the ridges. Then Tormentor whipped his pony around a boulder and disappeared. Randlett motioned for Abby to follow and in single file they rode through a cut into a grass valley with the sound of water echoing from one of the hills.

Before Randlett could move aside for Abby to pass, Tormentor had pinned the black against the ridge and the bold and stupid young brave had his hands in Abby's hair and was pulling her toward him.

She grimaced at the pain but as she fought to resist his biting kiss she raised a long whip-stick and slashed it across his face.

The brave's eyes tightened and he let go of her hair with an angry push. Hieeeeing! his pony, he turned and fled back through the narrow pass.

Randlett grinned and saluted. Then he realized she was shaking and he pointed the grey back into the cut.

Abby held up her hand to stop him. "I'm all right. Leave it be. Let's go."

Damping his anger, Randlett headed for the sound of the waterfall.

At the wall of cascading water that fell like a veil over the small pool, they sat their mounts in amazement. They stared at the melting snow that was funnelled along the higher buttes to tumble over the sharply jutting edge of rock fifty feet overhead. The water formed a fine spray of icy water eight feet wide, underneath it . . . behind it . . . was the opening to a prairie where the mesa sat in pristine majesty.

Randlett slid from the saddle and favoring his wounded

leg extracted a poncho and handed it to Abby. "Put this on. It'll keep you dry under that waterfall."

Abby dismounted with one hand to the small of her back, rubbing the stiff muscles. Neither of us is fit to tackle Fetty, Randlett thought and he gingerly stepped into the pool. Gasping at the sudden cold, he lowered himself into the water.

The shock sent his blood pounding. Teeth chattering, he forced himself to remain with his wounded leg submerged until the cold no longer seemed cold.

"Is that an old Cheyenne treatment for leg wounds?" Abby asked not knowing whether to be serious or not.

"As a matter of fact, yes," Randlett replied as he eased out onto the rocks. The water drained from his boots as he stomped beside her. "An icy swim fires up the circulation. Figured it might help this aching leg."

"Did it?"

"Stopped the pain and now it'll begin to heal. Maybe I'll not even need your famous liver tonic," he said with a wicked grin.

When he looked at her she was not smiling. She was staring at him with a strange stillness in her wide expectant eyes. Her face was glowing, lit by the pink fusion of dawn coming off the falling water. She looked tired and strained. But she was beautiful. His pulse beat wildly as he waited for her to pull away.

When she did not move he raised his hand and pushed the hood of the poncho off her head. His hand continued to move, it slid over the cowl of the hood, down the side of her face. Then his finger seemed to have a mind of its own. It touched her chin, wiping away satiny beads of water. Her lips trembled.

Then his hand swept to the back of her neck and he

drew her face toward him. Her lips on his, warm and yearning.

She leaned against him so that they swayed together. The beat of her heart matched his own.

Finally he let go, easing her away from him with his hand still on the back of her neck. He didn't trust his voice but it sounded normal as he said, "You could stay right here, not go into that meadow at all. You have your father to think about, you know."

"Yes, and I've been thinking. But Dad would understand. I have to go on."

"Yea . . . well, let's go then."

Chapter Twenty-seven

Tepee Mesa was a solitary mound of earth, a once molten upheaval of lava rock that was left dry and barren in the middle of a mountain park. It rose one hundred feet from a bed of wild grass and flowers. The sides were ribbed, deeply etched funnels of hard sandstone. A clump of stunted pinon pines and a mass of bushes adorned the top.

From his position near the falls Randlett studied the mound, wishing to peer into the nesting grounds of Leek Fetty. Movement far to the left caught his eye and he saw horses grazing near the foot of the mesa.

"We'd best hoof it from here," Randlett whispered, not chancing his voice to carry in the clear isolation of the mountain air. "We're sitting ducks as it is but maybe we'll be smaller ducks if we walk."

They dismounted, Abby hugging the rifle, Randlett touching the cartridge belt on his waist. They began a course that skirted in a semi-circle, avoiding a direct line from waterfall to mesa.

Stick-tights clung to Randlett's wet boots as he tromped a path through the thick growth. Beds of scarlet gilia and the delicate pale blue flowerets of wild flax grew in profusion. Occasionally the dying, yellow balsamroot sunflower poked up its tall head.

He began to sweat. The midday sun made a hotbed of the park. The ground was level and he did not expect either McPherson or Simon to be hidden in the grass, yet he kept an ear tuned for sounds and an eye raking the floor of the meadow. They had seen no one standing on the flat-topped edge of the mesa, no rifle shot had broken the silence. He prayed the two outlaws—and Simon—were holed up in the shade of those trees. And if the Blood had warned them, they would be waiting up there for an ambush.

Fifty feet from the foot of the mesa he palmed the Colt. The steeply vertical sides of the cliff told him there had to be a stairway. Either manmade or natural, but a special place for climbing to the top.

Motioning Abby to stay close, he began walking around the base of the tower. He found the entrance immediately. It was an ancient Indian footpath, hewn out by hand.

Eyes glued to the outlet a hundred feet up, Randlett bounded up the path. Quickly. Lightly.

As soon as his feet scooted in the dry red sand that covered the mesa's plateau, a man lunged out of the bushes on his left. Randlett was struck mid-gut, the wind swooshing out of his lungs. He fell backward near the edge, the Colt dropping with a dull thud into the sand.

Groggy for an instant, Randlett shook his head and strained to focus on his assailant. Soda McPherson staggered up in front of him. He seemed to sway. He stepped back with his hand fumbling for the gun in his holster.

He's wounded, Randlett thought, and as the old man fired he rolled toward his own gun, jerked it up and leveled it in one lightning move.

But something held his finger. Soda McPherson wiped a slobber of tobacco and thumbed the pistol in his hand to fire . . .

He missed by two feet. Hell! the man must be blind, Randlett muttered and he sprang at the old coot with a blow that knocked them both into the rocks. Randlett heard a nauseating crack as the bandit fell. McPherson groaned, tried to rise and slumped onto the ground with his ancient tobacco-stained hands clawing wildly in the dirt.

Randlett waited as Abby crawled over the edge. Instantly, rifle pointed, she hunkered on her heels covering the open area behind them in a series of swift turns. In the middle of the plateau the brush was thick, good cover for Fetty . . . and Simon.

Randlett nodded at McPherson who was crawling, not about to give up. "Watch him!" he whispered, then sprinted toward the grove of tall beeches directly in front of the low-growing bushes that must house the camp. He squatted near a gnarled tree trunk, pointing the forty-four toward the bushes.

"Simon!" he called and silence settled on the hill like death.

"Damn you, Fetty!" he yelled louder this time. "Come out and meet your due."

Salty sweat ran into Randlett's eyes and he wiped them with his sleeve. A slight shuffling noise came from the bushes and Randlett scooted to his right until he could see a gap in the heavy brush. Ah! The entrance.

He grinned stiffly and keeping low, he crabbed in the opposite direction . . . toward the back. When he had gone what he guessed to be half-way around the encirclement, he slithered between a brush clump and some of the thick-needled pines.

Closing in from that angle he scanned the open circle. He saw no one. There was no tent, only scattered bedding and a rock firepit. Then he saw Fetty's back. The outlaw was standing beside a large wooden crate. His arms were holding the shotgun . . . pointed at the opening between those bushes where Randlett would have stepped.

A ball of heat exploded in Randlett's chest as he saw that gun again . . . and that man. This time there would be no long drawn-out revenge fight. There would only be death.

Swallowing the sour knot rising in his throat, Randlett snarled through tight lips, "Not this time, Fetty!"

The man's back went ridged. He turned. The two guns fired as one. The shotgun spewed its pellets overhead a split second after the single forty-four slug tore a hole in the outlaw's chest.

The shotgun fell from the man's hands and the bandit slumped to the ground amid Abby's terrified, "No!"

Kane Randlett lowered his arm and a shiver trembled over his body. Fetty . . . Oh, Lord, the man was not Fetty.

All the blood drained from Randlett's face. He stumbled toward the fallen man. He stared. He could not take his eyes off the dark-haired young man lying on the ground. A young man who looked exactly like a grown-up Simon would look . . . a young man who looked just like his older brother, Kane.

Abby was crying, twisting her hand in her shirt tail. She gulped and sobbed and fell on her knees beside the man. "Simon," she muttered, "why . . . why are you here? What were you doing?"

A gurgle passed through the outlaw's lips and he strained to smile. "You . . . you look mighty pretty, Abby girl."

Her head dropped and curling into a ball she began to weep.

Randlett bent over the blood-damp body of his brother. There was no doubt now. There was proof. The shotgun had been in his hands. He had been ready, anxious, to kill the man he knew was his brother.

"Simon . . . what is this . . . how did this happen?"

A crooked, egotistical grin lit up the handsome face. The downed bandit turned his eyes away from Abby and looked at Kane. "You . . . you suckered me. . . ." He took a shaky breath and tried to raise his hand but it dropped into the dirt.

Randlett was amazed . . . disappointed . . . then a cold anger stilled his heart. He could not speak.

"You're a d . . . damn fool, Kane," Simon whispered. "Gave fair warning but you wouldn't leave it alone." Simon gasped and managed this time to lay his hand on his chest in the darkening pool. The bullet had hit center heart and Randlett could see there was no help for it. He asked in a cold, sharp voice, "Where's Fetty, Simon?"

Simon's dark-lashed eyelids swayed heavily, then opened wide. "Huh, you should know. You beat him up and left him."

"He's not with you?"

Simon's voice was bubbling now with starts and sputters. "We . . . left him with . . . his squaw, near dead. Hell, Kane, you have some whack in that arm o' yours. . . ."

Randlett wiped his mouth. "Simon . . . what happened? Why have you done this?"

Abby had kneeled beside them, her hand on Simon's

forehead. He smiled again and said, "Fetty had a good set-up, Kane. He was like a father to me. Taught me . . . gave me contacts. He was a man who knew how to get what he wanted and he showed me how.

"S . . . Sorry about Lon," he said with a drop in his voice as he gazed at Abby. "But as soon as Lon shot at me he recognized me. And o' course Fetty couldn't let that be."

Simon blinked and added, ". . . he nicked me too, that ol' codger."

Randlett spat to the side, his face trembling, his fist clenching. "What about our father, Simon?"

The dying man managed, "Give me a drink will you, girl?"

Abby went to get a canteen. Simon let the water dribble into his mouth, choked, then jerked his head aside and lay still. Randlett thought he was gone, but then a low bitter laugh poured from the sullen outlaw. "Our father!" he called out with anger rising in him like poison. "That whippet! He was a damn fool who couldn't do a damn thing right. Nearly got us killed carrying all that money with no guns. Wanting to open a school . . ." Simon coughed red spittle . . . "imagine that."

He chuckled then and turning his face away, quietly stopped breathing.

Randlet stood up. He gazed at the family ring that now adorned his middle finger. Putting it between his teeth he pulled it off, then laid it in Simon's open palm. He closed the blood-wet hand over it and said grimly, "Thought you had found the answer to the good life, didn't you kid? Pity, when all the time you had it right in your own hand."

Chapter Twenty-eight

They dug a shallow grave where he lay. They put the shotgun in beside him. There was no marker for his head and neither Abby nor Randlett felt like saying words over the grave.

A satchel of money had been carelessly stuffed among the outlaw's belongings. Abby picked it up mumbling about having a difficult time getting it back to the correct parties.

Randlett walked out of the trees to tend to Soda McPherson.

The old man was gone. Randlett whirled to search the mesa top. Seeing no one, his eye came back to the ground where the bandit had fallen. It was smudged in a wide circle, the hand and elbow prints, as well as heel gouges, indicating he had dragged himself to the edge of the plateau.

Randlett stepped to the ledge and peered down. McPherson was lodged in a crack half-way to the bottom. The body was limp and still. His back was broken.

* * *

"Kane," Abby asked as they lumbered down the last of the peaks, headed toward the rocks where they had left Sheriff Draper. "Then Simon led that last raid himself. . . ."

"Seems so," Randlett replied with a sick ache in his guts as he realized Simon had been the one to change tactics and come in West of the Rocks. Damn him, those two good hired men shouldn't have died! But then neither should all the others, Randlett mused, his eyes closing at the thought. Simon had quietly allowed Fetty to gun down Lon . . . and later with complete ease he had shot Stalking Deer . . . and would have killed Randlett himself if he hadn't been faster on the draw. Simon, Randlett concluded solemnly, you're not the little brother I lost out there on the plain after all.

Later Abby asked, "Why didn't we know, Kane?"

With a disgusted shake of his head Randlett said, "Huh, I don't know, Abby. Maybe love blinded both of us." That seemed to satisfy her and they said no more. Perhaps later they would talk about it, understand it better. But Randlett thought not. They each had been a part of Simon's lie, innocently drawn into the twisted, diabolical dream of the young traitor. That phase of their lives would be better forgotten.

They rode silently then, until they heard Sheriff Draper's hearty hello. He was alert, sitting up, and Randlett helped him onto one of the horses they had brought down from the Tepee.

A day later, at the road, as Abby and Draper pulled to one side, Randlett caught Abby's eye. "You understand don't you? Why I must do this?"

"Yes," she answered. A tentative smile flashed across her face, bringing a spark of life to her tired brow. Randlett was grateful for her understanding. As she kicked the black to follow Draper into Wolfe City he watched until her small upright figure disappeared from sight.

Randlett lifted the blanket-wrapped body of Tom Stalking Deer out of the notch of the oak tree, hefted it up and threw it over the back of another of the bandits' horses.

He moved like a sleepwalker. Mounting the gelding he started for the camp of the Cheyenne.

The burial took place during the next two days. Sun Woman and the other women prepared the returned hero's body with all the love and devotion and ceremony accorded the greatest brave. And of course after hearing that Stalking Deer had fought the bandits about to kill the white friend of Randlett, and had died giving his life for her . . . he had indeed become a hero.

Food was lavishly prepared. Food which they could not afford but which they were bound to fix.

Sun Woman herself and Magpie were fasting. Sun Woman was a mother who had lived so long with dreams and wishes for her son that the death of Stalking Deer was merely a part of that dream. She gravely accepted his death without undue grief. But Randlett knew she would age ten years in the next few days.

Magpie's reaction was more traumatic. She sat for long hours crying and rocking, reliving all their lovely childhood days. The youthful days when they believed in the future. When they accepted one another and the love they had for one another without fear.

The days went slowly for Randlett. Activity, talk and seeing the others in their sorrow helped during the day. But at night, sleeping again in the lodge where he and

Stalking Deer had so often slept side by side, he felt depressed and restless.

The Indian had come close to forsaking the spirit of integrity that his heritage had given him when he thought he saw his white brother grow taller and become stronger and gain favor with the girl he loved. Then Stalking Deer had taken that silly, civilized name in order to become a part of that other, "better" world. Tom, he called himself. Randlett smiled sadly at the memory. Stalking Deer had wanted to be called Tom Stalking Deer. Randlett thought of the many times he and Magpie had deliberately left off the white-man name, letting Stalking Deer sulk or become angry. Randlett was glad the issue of his name had been reconciled.

On the third day as he was getting ready to leave, Stands Around asked for a meeting. The aging chief sat for an hour and smoked his pipe, making occasional grunts or comments about unimportant things before he finally brought up the real subject of his meeting. "You have brought back the bones of a brave son to lie in the sacred ground, not to be lost and eaten by wolves or the grizzly. Stalking Deer died in battle . . . in honor . . . that has erased all the evil past. And you have given him back to his mother."

Randlett remained quiet, having an inkling of what was to come . . . and wishing it wouldn't.

"For this you may have the daughter of Fair Wind as your wife."

Randlett blew smoke to the side and put down the pipe. He chose his words carefully.

"My father, Chief of these Cheyenne people, I am honored. It would please me to stay and lodge here forever . . . to take Magpie for my wife." As he said this Randlett knew it was true. A part of him wanted nothing more. A part of him loved this simple, quiet, long-suffering people. And it would be easy to accept it. To make Magpie his wife. To raise healthy brown-skinned little boys. He could so easily forget he was ever anything but Indian.

As short a time as three weeks ago he might have done this. But now there was Abby and he knew he loved her as he could never love Magpie. And with a sudden sense of fierce pride he remembered his real father. That scholar, teacher, man who had a dream to give of himself to others, thinking he had a debt to teach this new world at the risk of his own death and ruin.

Such an inheritance would be hard to uphold and one Randlett had long thought he could never fulfill. Now he desperately wanted to try.

"But, my father," Randlett continued, "I am a man of two peoples. And for my life to become whole I must seek to know that other life. The name of my white father must be honored even as the name of my Indian father has been."

Walks Around blinked against the heavy smoke rising from the pit. He said nothing but began wagging first his head and then his body, back and forth, in sad, fateful agreement.

Kane Randlett took the flannel head band from his pocket and tied it around his forehead again. The old man was pleased.

Randlett left then, saddled the grey and rode out at a slow walk.

A long, low, barren hill rose on his right and from it he could hear the plaintive song of Magpie. His heart ached for her and he felt an unbearable agony as he passed. He knew she was grieving, crying out for Stalking Deer . . . and for the young Kane Randlett . . . and for herself.

And he knew even as he and Stalking Deer had once begun the mourning of their friend long ago . . . that she too had begun her mourning by cutting four long gashes down a line on the innermost side of her lovely right arm.

The serene call of a bob-white floated across the meadow in front of the McMillan ranch house. Abby smiled with closed eyes as Kane Randlett picked up her hand and pressed it to his lips.

They were sitting on the porch swing, contented without talking, savoring the quiet and promise of the evening.

"How long will you be gone," she finally asked.

"Just long enough to find the gold Pa hid on that rabbit ear of a mountain. Now that I think about it, I believe I know exactly where he would have put it. There was a deep indention 'round the left side with any number of rock crannies to stash a treasure in.

"Don't worry, I'll find it."

"I don't need it, Kane, if you're thinking of getting it for me."

He squeezed her hand. "I know that. I need it for Pa. I intend to use at least part of it to build that school house he wanted. And maybe some of it for a few cattle . . . to start a herd of my own."

When she turned away he pulled her chin back around toward him and added, ". . . a herd of our own."

"That's better," she said and accepted a kiss.